VJS

D0359481

The FAMOUS FIVE *are*
Julian, Dick, George (Georgina by rights),
Anne, and Timmy the dog

Spending their holiday on a farm in Cornwall,
the Five vow that if an adventure comes along,
they will turn their backs on it.
But they find it very difficult to keep this vow
when they learn that a light has been seen on
stormy nights, shining from the ruined
Wreckers' Tower.

This is the Five's twelfth adventure

Enid Blyton

Five go down
to the sea

Illustrated by Betty Maxey

KNIGHT BOOKS
Hodder and Stoughton

ISBN 0 340 04251 6

Illustrations copyright © 1974 Hodder & Stoughton Ltd

First published in 1953
This edition first published 1969
Thirteenth impression 1978

Printed and bound in Great Britain for
Hodder and Stoughton Paperbacks, a division of
Hodder and Stoughton Ltd, Mill Road, Dunton Green,
Sevenoaks, Kent (Editorial Office: 47 Bedford Square,
London WC1 3DP) by Cox & Wyman Ltd,
London, Reading and Fakenham

This book is sold subject to the condition that it shall not by
way of trade or otherwise be lent, resold, hired out or
otherwise circulated without the publisher's prior consent in
any form of binding or cover other than that in which this
is published and without a similar condition including this
condition being imposed on the subsequent purchaser.

CONTENTS

Chapter One

THE HOLIDAY BEGINS

'Blow! I've got a puncture!' said Dick. 'My tyre's going flat. Worst time it could possibly happen!'

Julian glanced down at Dick's back tyre. Then he looked at his watch. 'You've just got time to pump it up and hope for the best,' he said. 'We've got seven minutes before the train goes.'

Dick jumped off and took his pump. The others got off their bicycles, too, and stood round, watching to see if the tyre blew up well or not.

They were on their way to Kirrin Station to catch the train, bicycles and all. Their luggage had gone on in advance, and they thought they had left plenty of time to ride to the station, get their bicycles labelled and put in the luggage van, and catch the train comfortably.

'We *can't* miss the train!' said George, putting on her best scowl. She always hated it when things went wrong.

'We can. Easiest thing in the world!' said Julian, grinning at George's fierce face. 'What do *you* say, Timmy?'

Timmy barked sharply, as if to say he certainly agreed. He licked George's hand and she patted him. The scowl left her face as she saw Dick's tyre coming up well. They'd just do it! Dick felt his tyre, gave a sigh of relief, and put his pump back in its place.

'Phew! That was hot work,' he said, mounting his bicycle. Hope it will last till we get to the station. I was afraid you'd have to go without me.'

'Oh, *no*,' said Anne. 'We'd have caught the next train. Come on, Timmy!'

The four cousins and Timmy the dog raced on towards the station. They cycled into the station yard just as the signal went up to show the train was due. The porter came towards them, his big round face red and smiling.

'I sent your luggage off for you,' he said. 'Not much between you, I must say – just one small trunk!'

'Well, we don't wear much on holidays,' said Julian. 'Can you label our bikes quickly for us? I see the train is due.'

The porter began to label the four bicycles. He didn't hurry. He wouldn't let the train go off again till he had done his job, that was certain. There it was now, coming round the bend.

'You going off to Cornwall, I see?' said the porter. 'And to Tremannon, too. You want to be careful of bathing there. That's a fierce coast and a hungry sea.'

'Oh, do you know it?' said Anne, surprised. 'Is it a nice place?'

'Nice? Well, I dunno about that,' said the porter,

raising his voice as the train came rumbling in. 'I used to go out in my uncle's fishing-boat all round there, and it's wild and lonely. I shouldn't have thought it was much of a place for a holiday – no pier, no ice-cream sellers, no concert parties, no cinema, no . . .'

'Good,' said Julian. 'We can do without all those, thank you. We mean to bathe, and hire a boat, and fish, and bike all round about. That's *our* kind of holiday!'

'Woof!' said Timmy, wagging his tail.

'Yes, and yours too,' said George, rubbing his big head. 'Come on, we'd better get into a carriage.'

'I'll see to your bikes,' said the porter. 'Have a good holiday, and if you see my uncle, tell him you know me. His name's same as mine, John Polpenny.'

'"By Tre, Pol and Pen, you may know the Cornish-men",' quoted Julian, getting into a carriage with the others. 'Thanks John. We'll look up your uncle if we can!'

They each took a corner seat, and Timmy went to the opposite door, put his feet up on the ledge and his nose out of the window. He meant to stand like that all the way! He loved the rush of air past his nose.

'Timmy, come down,' said George.

Timmy took no notice. He was happy. It was holi-days again, and he was with everybody he loved. They were going away together. There might be rabbits to chase. Timmy had never yet caught a rabbit, but he went on hoping!

'Now, we're off again!' said Julian, settling into his

corner. 'Gosh, how I do like the beginnings of a holiday, getting ready, looking at maps, planning how to get there, and then at last setting off!'

'On a lovely fine day like this!' said Anne. 'George, how did your mother hear of Tremannon Farm?'

'Well, it was Father who heard about it, really,' said George. 'You know Father's got a lot of scientist friends who like to go off to lonely places and work out all kinds of ideas in peace and quiet. Well, one of them went to Tremannon Farm because he heard it was one of the quietest places in the country. Father said his friend went there all skin and bone and came back as fat as a Christmas goose, and Mother said that sounded *just* the place for us to go to these hols!'

'She's right!' said Dick. 'I feel a bit skin-and-bonish myself after slaving at school for three months. I could do with fattening up!'

They all laughed. 'You may *feel* skin-and-bonish, but you don't look it,' said Julian. 'You want a bit of exercise to take your fat off. We'll get it, too. We'll walk and bike and bathe and climb . . .'

'And eat,' said George. 'Timmy, you must be polite to the farm dogs, or you'll have a bad time.'

'And you must remember that when you go out to play, you'll have to ask the other dogs' permission before you can chase their rabbits,' said Dick solemnly.

Timmy thumped his tail against Dick's knees and opened his mouth to let his tongue hang out. He looked exactly as if he were laughing.

'That's right. Grin at my jokes,' said Dick. 'I'm

glad you're coming, Tim, it would be awful without you.'

'He always *has* come with us, on every holiday,' said George. 'And he's shared in every single adventure we've ever had.'

'Good old Timmy,' said Julian. 'Well, he may share in one this time, too. You never know.'

'I'm not going to have any adventures this time,' said Anne in a firm voice. 'I just want a holiday, nothing more. Let's have a jolly good time, and not go on looking for anything strange or mysterious or adventurous.'

'Right,' said Julian. 'Adventures are *off* this time. Definitely off. And if anything does turn up, we pooh-pooh it and walk off. Is that agreed?'

'Yes,' said Anne.

'All right,' said George, doubtfully.

'Fine,' said Dick.

Julian looked surprised. 'Gosh, you're a poor lot, I must say. Well, I'll fall in with you, if you're all agreed. Even if we find ourselves right in the very middle of Goodness Knows What, we say "No, thank you" and walk away. That's agreed.'

'Well,' began George, 'I'm not sure if . . .' But what she wasn't sure about nobody knew because Timmy chose that moment to fall off the seat. He yelped as he hit the floor with a bang, and immediately went back to his post at the window, putting his head right out.

'We'll have to get him in and shut the windows,' said George. 'He might get something in his eye.'

'No. I'm not going to cook slowly to a cinder in this hot carriage with all the windows shut, not even for the sake of Timmy's eyes,' said Julian, firmly. 'If you can't make him obey you and come inside, he can jolly well get something in his eye.'

However, the problem was solved very quickly because at that moment the train gave a most unearthly shriek and disappeared headlong into utter blackness. Timmy, astounded, fell back into the carriage and tried to get on to George's knee, terrified.

'Don't be a baby, Timmy,' said George. 'It's only a tunnel! Ju, haul him off me. It's too hot to try and nurse a heavy dog like Timmy. Stop it, Timmy, I tell you it's only a *tunnel*!'

The journey seemed very long. The carriage was so hot, and they had to change twice. Timmy panted loudly and hung his tongue out; George begged the porters for water at each changing-place.

They had their lunch with them, but somehow they weren't hungry. They got dirtier and dirtier, and thirstier and thirstier, for they very quickly drank the orangeade they had brought with them.

'Phew!' said Julian, fanning himself with a magazine. 'What wouldn't I give for a bathe? Timmy, don't pant all over me. You make me feel hotter still.'

'What time do we get there?' asked Anne.

'Well, we have to get out at Polwilly Halt,' said Julian. 'That's the nearest place to Tremannon Farm. We bike from there. With luck, we should be there by tea-time.'

'We ought to have brought masses more to drink,' said Dick. 'I feel like a man who's been lost in a sun-scorched desert for weeks.'

They were all extremely glad when they at last arrived at Polwilly Halt. At first they didn't think it was a halt, but it was. It was nothing but a tiny wooden stage built beside the railway. The children sat and waited. They hadn't even seen the little wooden stage or the small sign that said 'Polwilly Halt'.

The sound of impatient feet came along the little platform. The guard's perspiring face appeared at the window.

'Well? Didn't you want to get out here? You going to sit there all day?'

'Gosh! Is this Polwilly?' said Julian, leaping up. 'Sorry. We didn't know it was a Halt. We'll be out in half a tick.'

The train started off almost before they had banged the door. They stood there on the funny little staging, all alone save for their four bicycles at the other end. The little Halt seemed lonely and lost, set in the midst of rolling fields and rounded hills. Not a building was in sight!

But not far off to the west George's sharp eyes saw something lovely. She pulled Julian's arm. 'Look, the sea! Over there, between the hills, in the dip. Can't you see it? I'm sure it's the sea. What a heavenly blue.'

'It's always that gorgeous blue on the Cornish coast,' said Dick. 'Ah, I feel better when I see that. Come on, let's get our bikes and find our way to Tremannon Farm. If I don't get something to drink soon I shall certainly hang my tongue out, like Timmy.'

They went to get their bikes. Dick felt his back tyre. It was a bit soft, but not too bad. He could easily pump it up again. 'How far is it to Tremannon Farm?' he asked.

Julian looked at his notes. '"Get out at Polwilly Halt. Then bike four miles to Tremannon Farm, along narrow lanes. Tremannon Village is about one mile before you get to the farm." Not too bad. We might get some lemonade, or even an ice-cream, in the village.'

'Woof, woof,' said Timmy, who knew the word ice-cream very well indeed.

'Poor Tim!' said Anne. 'He'll be so hot running beside our bikes. We'd better go slowly.'

'Well, if anyone thinks I'm going to tear along, he can think again,' said Dick. 'I'll go as slowly as you like, Anne!'

They set off with Timmy down a queer little lane, deep-set between high hedges. They went slowly for Timmy's sake. He panted along valiantly. Good old Timmy! He would never give up as long as he was with the four children.

It was about five o'clock and a very lovely evening. They met nobody at all, not even a slow old farm cart. It was even too hot for the birds to sing. No wind blew. There seemed a curious silence and loneliness everywhere.

Julian looked back at the other three with a grin. 'Adventure is in the air! I feel it. We're all set for adventure! But no, we'll turn our backs on it and say: "Away with you!" That's agreed!'

Chapter Two

TREMANNON FARM

IT certainly was a lovely ride to Tremannon Farm. Poppies blew by the wayside in hundreds, and honeysuckle threw its scent out from the hedges as they passed. The corn stood high in the fields, touched with gold already, and splashed with the scarlet of the poppies.

They came to Tremannon Village at last. It was really nothing but a winding street, set with a few shops and houses, and beyond that, straggling out, were other houses. Farther off, set in the hills, were a few farm-houses, their grey stone walls gleaming in the sun.

The four children found the general store and went in. 'Any ice-cream?' said Julian hopefully. But there was none. What a blow! There was orangeade and lemonade, however, quite cool through being kept down in the cellar of the store.

'You be the folks that old Mrs Penruthlan be having in?' said the village shopkeeper. 'She do be expecting of you. Furriners, bain't you?'

'Well, not exactly,' said Julian, remembering that to many Cornish folk anyone was a foreigner who did not belong to Cornwall. 'My mother had a great-aunt who lived in Cornwall all her life. So we're not *exactly* "furriners", are we?'

'You're furriners all right,' said the bent little shop-keeper, looking at Julian with bird-like eyes. 'Your talk is furrin-like, too. Like that man Mrs Penruthlan had before. We reckoned he was mad, though he was harmless enough.'

'Really?' said Julian, pouring himself out a third lemonade. 'Well, he was a scientist, and if you're going to be a really *good* one you have to be a bit mad, you know. At least, so I've heard. Golly, this lemonade is good. Can I have another bottle, please?'

The old woman suddenly laughed, sounding just like an amused hen. 'Well, well, Marty Penruthlan's got a fine meal ready for you, but seems like you won't be able to eat a thing, not with all that lemonade splashing about in your innards!'

'Don't say you can hear the splashing,' said Julian earnestly. 'Very bad manners, that! Furriners' manners, I'm sure. Well, how much do we owe you? That was jolly good lemonade.'

He paid the bill and they all mounted their bicycles once more, having been given minute directions as to how to get to the farm. Timmy set off with them, feeling much refreshed, having drunk steadily for four minutes without stopping.

'I should think you've had about as much water as would fill a horse-trough, Timmy,' Julian told him. 'My word, if this weather holds we're going to look like Red Indians!'

It was an uphill ride to Tremannon Farm, but they got there at last. As they cycled through the open gates, a fusillade of barks greeted them, and four large dogs came flying to meet them. Timmy put up his hackles at once and growled warningly. He went completely stiff, and stood there glaring.

A woman came out behind the dogs, her face one large smile. 'Now, Ben; now, Bouncer! Here, Nellie, here! Bad dog, Willy! It's all right, children, that's their way of saying "Welcome to Tremannon Farm!"'

The dogs now stood in a ring round the four children, their tongues out, their tails wagging vigorously. They were lovely dogs, three collies and one small black Scottie. Timmy eyed them one by one. George had her hand on his collar, just in case he should feel foolhardy all of a sudden and imagine he could take on all four dogs single-handed.

But he didn't. He behaved like a perfect gentleman! His tail wagged politely, and his hackles went down. The little Scottie ran up to him and sniffed his nose. Timmy sniffed back, his tail wagging more vigorously.

Then the three sheepdogs ran up, beautiful collies with plumy tails, and the children heaved sighs of relief to see that the farm dogs evidently were not going to regard Timmy as a 'furriner'!

'They're all right now,' said Mrs Penruthlan. 'They've introduced themselves to one another. Now come along with me. You must be tired and dirty – and hungry and thirsty. I've high tea waiting for you.'

She didn't talk in the Cornish way. She was pleased

to see them and gave them a grand welcome. She took them upstairs to a bathroom, big but primitive. There was one tap only and that was for cold water. It ran very slowly indeed!

But it was really cold, and was lovely and soft to wash in. The tired children cleaned themselves and combed their hair.

They had two bedrooms between them, one for the girls and one for the boys. They were rather small, with little windows that gave a meagre amount of light, so that the rooms looked dark even in the bright evening sunshine.

They were bare little rooms, with two beds in each, one chair, one chest of drawers, one cupboard and two small rugs. Nothing else! But, oh! the views out of the windows!

Miles and miles of countryside, set with cornfields, pasture land, tall hedges and glimpses of winding lanes; heather was out on some of the hills, blazing purple in the sun; and, gleaming in the distance was the dark blue brilliance of the Cornish sea. Lovely!

'We'll bike to the sea as soon as we can,' said Dick, trying to flatten the few hairs that would stick up straight on the top of his head. 'There are caves on this coast. We'll explore them. I wonder if Mrs Penruthlan would give us picnic lunches so that we can go off for the day when we want to.'

'Sure to,' said Julian. 'She's a pet. I've never felt so welcome in my life. Are we ready? Come on down, then. I'm beginning to feel very empty indeed.'

The high tea that awaited them was truly magnificent. A huge ham gleaming as pink as Timmy's tongue; a salad fit for a king. In fact, as Dick said, fit for *several* kings, it was so enormous. It had in it everything that anyone could possibly want.

'Lettuce, tomatoes, onions, radishes, mustard and cress, carrot grated up – that *is* carrot, isn't it, Mrs Penruthlan?' said Dick. 'And lashings of hard-boiled eggs.'

There was an enormous tureen of new potatoes, all gleaming with melted butter, scattered with parsley. There was a big bottle of home-made salad cream.

'Look at that cream cheese, too,' marvelled Dick, quite overcome. 'And that fruit cake. And are those drop-scones, or what? Are we supposed to have something of everything, Mrs Penruthlan?'

'Oh, yes,' said the plump little woman, smiling at Dick's pleasure. 'And there's a cherry tart made with our own cherries, and our own cream with it. I know what hungry children are. I've had seven of my own, all married and gone away. So I have to make do with other people's when I can get them.'

'I'm jolly glad you happened to get hold of *us*,' said Dick, beginning on ham and salad. 'Well, we'll keep you busy, Mrs Penruthlan. We've all got big appetites!'

'Ah, I've not met any children yet that could eat like mine,' said Mrs Penruthlan, sounding really sorry. 'Same as I've not met any man that can eat like Mr Penruthlan. He's a fine eater, he is. He'll be in soon.'

'I hope we shall leave enough for him,' said Anne, looking at the ham and the half-empty salad dish. 'No wonder my uncle's friend, the man who came to stay here, went away as fat as butter, Mrs Penruthlan.'

'Oh, the poor man!' said their hostess, who was now filling up their glasses with rich, creamy milk. 'Thin as my husband's old rake, he was, and all his bones showing and creaking. He said "No" to this and "No" to that, but I took no notice of him at all. If he didn't eat his dinner, I'd take his tray away and tidy it up, and then in ten minutes I'd take it back again and say: "Dinner-time, sir, and I hope you're hungry!" And he'd start all over again, and maybe that time he'd really tuck in!'

'But didn't he know you'd already taken him his dinner-tray once?' said Julian, astonished. 'Goodness, he *must* have been a dreamer.'

'I took his tray in three times once,' said Mrs Penruthlan. 'So you be careful in case I do the same kind of thing to you!'

'I should love it!' grinned Julian. 'Yes, please, I'd like some more ham. *And* more salad.'

Footsteps came outside the room, on the stone floor of the hall. The door opened and the farmer himself came in. The children stared at him in awe.

He was a strange and magnificent figure of a man – tall, well over six feet, broadly built, and as dark as a sunburnt Spaniard. His mane of hair was black and curly, and his eyes were as black as his hair.

'This is Mr Penruthlan,' said his wife, and the

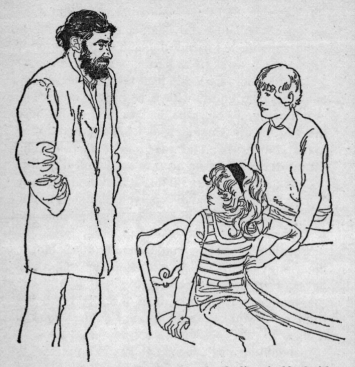

children stood up to shake hands, feeling half afraid
of this dark giant.

He nodded his head and shook hands. His hand was
enormous, and was covered with hairs so thick and
black that it was like fur. Anne felt that it would be
quite nice and soft to stroke, like a cat's back!'

He didn't say a word, but sat down and let his wife
serve him. 'Well, Mr Penruthlan,' she said, 'and how's
the cow getting along?'

'Ah,' said the farmer, taking a plate of ham. The children gazed at the slices in awe, seven or eight of them. Goodness!

'Oh, I'm glad she's all right,' said Mrs Penruthlan, stacking up some dirty plates. 'And is the calf a dear little thing – and what's the colour!'

'Ah,' said Mr Penruthlan, nodding his head.

'Red and white, like its mother! That's good, isn't it?' said his wife, who seemed to have a miraculous way of interpreting his 'Ahs'. 'What shall we call it?'

Everyone badly wanted to say 'Ah', but nobody dared. However, Mr Penruthlan didn't say 'Ah' that time, but something that sounded like 'Ock'.

'Yes, we'll call it Buttercup, then,' said his wife, nodding her head. 'You always have such good ideas, Mr Penruthlan.'

It sounded odd to hear her call her husband by his surname like that, and yet, somehow, the children couldn't imagine this giant of a fellow even *owning* a name like Jack or Jim. They went on with their own meal, enjoying every minute of it, watching Mr Penruthlan shovel in great mouthfuls, and working his way quickly through every dish. Mrs Penruthlan saw them watching him.

'He's a grand eater, isn't he?' she said, proudly. 'So were all my children. When they were at home, I was kept really busy, but now, with only Mr Penruthlan to feed, I feel quite lost. That's why I like people here. You'll tell me if you don't have enough to eat, won't you?'

They all laughed, and Timmy barked. He had had a wonderful meal, too; it was the remains of Mrs Penruthlan's big stock-pot, and was very tasty indeed. He had also got the largest bone he had ever had in his life. The only thing that really worried the well-fed Timmy now was, where could he put the bone out of the way of the farmdogs?

Mr Penruthlan suddenly made a peculiar noise and began undoing a trouser pocket at the back. 'Oo-ah!'

he said, and brought out a dirty, folded piece of paper. He handed it to his wife, who unfolded it and read it. She looked up at the children, smiling.

'Now, *here's* a bit of excitement!' she said. 'The Barnies will be along this week! You'll love them.'

'What *are* the Barnies?' asked George, puzzled at Mrs Penruthlan's evident pleasure and excitement.

'Oh, they're travelling players that wander round the countryside and play and act in our big barns,' said Mrs Penruthlan. 'We've no cinemas for miles, you know, so the Barnies are always very welcome.'

'Oh, you call them Barnies because they use your barns for their shows,' said Anne, seeing light. 'Yes, we shall love to see them, Mrs Penruthlan. Will they play in *your* barn?'

'Yes. We'll have all the village here when the Barnies come,' said Mrs Penruthlan, her cheeks going red with delight. 'And maybe people from Trelin Village, too. Now, there's a treat for you!'

'Ah,' said Mr Penruthlan, and nodded his great head. Evidently he liked the Barnies, too. He gave a sudden laugh and said something short and quite incomprehensible.

'He says you'll like Clopper the horse,' said his wife, laughing. 'The things he does! The way he sits down and crosses his legs. Well, you wait and see. That horse!'

This sounded rather astonishing. A horse that sat down and crossed its legs? Julian winked at Dick. They would most certainly see the Barnies!

Chapter Three

THE FIRST EVENING

AFTER their wonderful high tea the four children
didn't really feel like doing very much. Dick thought
he ought to mend his puncture, but wasn't sure that
he could bend over properly!

Mrs Penruthlan began to stack the dishes and clear
away. George and Anne offered to help her. 'Well,
that's kind of you, Anne and Georgina,' said the farmer's wife. 'But you're tired tonight. You can give me
a hand some other time. By the way, which of you is
which?'

'I'm Anne,' said Anne.

'And I'm George, not Georgina,' said George. 'So
please don't call me that. I hate it. I always wanted to
be a boy, so I only like to be called George.'

'What she really means is that she won't answer unless you *do* call her George,' said Anne. 'Well, if you
really are sure you don't need our help, we'll go out
with the boys.'

So out they went, George really looking far more
like a boy than a girl, with her grey jeans and shirt
and her short, curly hair and freckled face. She put her
hands in her pockets and tried to walk like Dick!

Dick soon found his puncture and mended it. Mr

Penruthlan came by with some straw for his cow and new calf. The boys watched him in awe, for he was carrying almost a wagon load of straw tied up in bales! What strength he had! He nodded to them and passed without a word.

'Why doesn't he talk?' wondered Dick. 'I suppose all his seven children take after their talkative mother, and he never had a chance to get a word in. And it's too late now, he's forgotten how to!'

They laughed. 'What a giant of a man,' said Julian. 'I hope I grow as big as that.'

'I don't. I'd hate to have my bare feet poking out of the bottom of the bed every night,' said Dick. 'There. I've finished that puncture. See the nail that made it? I must have run over it on the way to the station this morning.'

'Do look at Timmy,' said Julian. 'He's having the time of his life with those farm dogs, acting just like a puppy!'

So he was, bounding here and there, rushing round the dogs and then rushing away, jumping on first one and then another, till they all went down in an excited, yapping scrum, the little Scottie doing his best to keep up with everything!

'Timmy's going to have a good time here,' said Dick. 'And he'll soon lose his beautiful waist-line if he eats as well as we do!'

'We'll take him on long bike rides,' said Julian. 'He can't grow much tummy if he runs for miles!'

The girls came up just then. A few feet behind

trotted a queer little boy, bare-footed, shock-headed and very dirty.

'Who's this?' said Dick.

'I don't know,' said George. 'He suddenly appeared behind us and has been following us ever since. He just won't go away!'

The boy wore a ragged pair of jeans and an old pullover. He was black-eyed and burnt dark-brown by the sun. He stood a few feet away and stared.

'Who are you?' said Dick. The boy went back a few steps in fright. He shook his head.

'I said, who are you?' said Dick again. 'Or, if you prefer it another way, what's your name?'

'Yan,' said the boy.

'Yan?' said Dick. 'That's a queer name.'

'He probably means *Jan*,' said George.

The boy nodded. 'Iss. Yan,' he said.

'I suppose "Iss" means "Yes",' said Anne. 'All right, Jan. You can go now.'

'I stay,' said the boy solemnly. 'Iss.'

And stay he did, following them about everywhere, gazing at all they did with the utmost curiosity, as if he had never in his life seen children before!

'He's like a mosquito,' said Dick. 'Always buzzing around. I'm getting tired of it. Hey, Yan!'

'Iss?'

'Clear out now! Understand? Get away, go, run off, vamoose, bunk, scoot!' explained Dick sternly. Yan stared.

Mrs Penruthlan came out and heard all this. 'Jan

bothering you?' she said. 'He's as full of curiosity as a cat. Go home, Jan. Take this to your old Grandad. And here's some for you.'

Jan came up eagerly and took the packet of food Mrs Penruthlan held out to him, and the slice of cake. He ran off without a word, his bare feet making no sound.

'Who is he?' asked George. 'What a little scarecrow!'

'He's a poor little thing,' said the farmer's wife. 'He's got no kith or kin except for his old great-grandad, and there's more than eighty years between them! The old man is our shepherd. Do you see that hill over there, well, he's got a hut on the other side, and there he lives, winter and summer alike, and that child with him.'

'Surely he ought to go to school?' said Julian. 'Perhaps he does?'

'No,' said Mrs Penruthlan. 'He plays truant nearly all the time. You ought to go and talk to his old great-grandad. His father was one of the Wreckers on this coast, and he can tell you some strange stories about those dreadful days.'

'We'll certainly go and talk to him,' said Dick. 'I'd forgotten that this Cornish coast was the haunt of Wreckers. They shone false lights to bring ships in close to shore, so that they would be smashed to pieces on the rocks, didn't they?'

'Yes, and then they robbed the poor, groaning ship when she was helpless,' said Mrs Penruthlan. 'And it's said they paid no heed to the drowning folk, either. Those were wicked days.'

'How far is it to cycle to the sea?' said George. 'I can see it from my bedroom window.'

'Oh, it won't take you more than ten minutes,' said the farmer's wife. 'Go tomorrow, if you like. You all look very tired now. Why don't you take a short walk and go to bed? I'll have a snack ready for you when you come in.'

'Oh, we couldn't *possibly* eat any more tonight, thank you,' said Dick, hurriedly. 'But the walk is quite a good idea. We'd like to see round the farm.'

Mrs Penruthlan left them, and Dick looked round at the others. 'A snack!' he said. 'I never thought I'd groan at the thought. But I bet Mr Penruthlan will want a jolly good snack when he comes in. Come on, let's go up by those sheds.'

They went off together, Timmy following behind with his four friends, their tails wagging amiably. It was still a lovely evening, and a cool breeze came down from the hills, making it lovelier still. The children wandered round, enjoying the familiar farm sights, the ducks on the pond, a few hens still clucking round, the grey sheep dotting the hills. Cows were peacefully grazing and an old farm horse came to a gate to stare at them.

They rubbed his velvety nose, and he bent down to sniff at Timmy, whom he didn't know. Timmy sniffed solemnly back.

They went into the barns and looked around, big,

dark, sweet-smelling places, stored with many things. Dick was sure that the biggest one would be the one used by the Barnies. What fun!

'I bet they'll be pretty awful, but good fun, all the same,' he said. 'It must be grand to wander round the countryside with all your belongings done up in a parcel or two, and then amaze the country people with your songs and dances and acting. I wouldn't mind trying it myself! I'm pretty good at a spot of conjuring, for instance!'

'Yes, you are,' said Anne. 'Wouldn't it be fun if we could give a little show too, if the Barnies would let us join them just for one evening?'

'We wouldn't be allowed to because we're "furriners",' said Dick, grinning. 'I say, what's that, over there, behind that sack?'

Timmy at once went to see, and stood there barking. The others went over to look.

'It's that kid Yan again,' said Julian in disgust. He pulled the boy out from his hiding-place. 'What are you following us around for, you little idiot?' he demanded. 'We don't like it. See? Go and find your old Grandad before you eat all the food Mrs Penruthlan gave you. Go on, now.'

He pushed the boy out of the barn, and watched him go into the next field. 'That's got rid of him,' he said. 'I think he's a bit simple. We'll go and see that Grandad of his one day and see if he really *has* got anything interesting to say about the old Wreckers.'

'Let's go back now,' said Dick, yawning. 'I've seen enough of this place to know I'm going to like it a lot. I'm going to like my bed tonight too. Coming, Ju?'

They all felt the same as Dick. His yawn had set them yawning, too, and they thought longingly of bed. They made their way back to the farm, followed closely by Timmy at their heels, and the other four dogs a respectful distance away.

They said good night to the two Penruthlans, who were sitting peacefully listening to their radio. Mrs Penruthlan wanted to come up with them but they wouldn't let her.

They said good night to the farmer, who grunted

'Ah!' without even looking at them, and went on listening to the radio programme. Then up the stairs they went, and into their rooms.

When Julian was in bed and almost asleep he heard a scrabbling noise outside his window. He half-opened his eyes, and listened. He hoped it wasn't rats! If it was, Anne would probably hear them too, and be scared, and Timmy would hear them and bark the place down!

The scrabbling noise came again. Julian spoke softly to Dick. 'Dick! Are you awake? Did you hear that noise at the window?'

No answer. Dick was sound asleep, dreaming that he had a puncture in his foot and couldn't walk till it was mended! Julian lay and listened. Yes, there it was again, and now surely there was someone trying to peep in at the tiny window?

He slid out of bed and went to the side of the window. Thick ivy grew outside. Somebody was still there for Julian could see the leaves shaking.

He put his head suddenly out of the window, and a scared face, quite close to his, stared in fright.

'Yan! What do you think you're doing?' said Julian, fiercely. 'I'll spank you if you go on like this, staring and peeping! What's so queer about us?'

Yan was terrified. He suddenly slithered down the ivy like a cat, landed with a slight thud on the ground and then ran off into the twilight at top speed.

'I hope he's not going to follow us around all the time,' thought Julian, getting into bed again. 'I'll teach him a lesson if he does. Blow him! Now he's made me wide awake!'

But it wasn't long before Julian was sleeping as soundly as Dick. Neither of them stirred until a cock outside their window decided that it was time the whole world woke up, and crowed at the top of his voice.

'Cock-a-doodle-DOO!'

The boys woke with a jump. The early sun streamed into the room, and Julian glanced at his watch. How early it was! And yet he could hear movements downstairs that told him Mrs Penruthlan was up and about, and so was her giant of a husband.

He fell asleep again, and was awakened by a loud knock at his door, and Mrs Penruthlan's voice. 'It's half past seven, and breakfast will be on the table for you at eight. Wake up!'

How lovely to wake in a strange place at the beginning of a holiday, to think of bathing and biking and picnicking and eating and drinking, forgetting all about exams and rules and punishments! The four children and Timmy stretched themselves and stared at the sunshine outside. What a day!

Downstairs breakfast awaited them. 'Super!' said Dick, eyeing the bacon and fried eggs, the cold ham, and the home-made jam and marmalade. 'Mrs Penruthlan, your seven children must have been very sorry to marry and leave home. I feel, if I'd been one of them, I'd have stayed with you for the rest of my life!'

Chapter Four

DOWN IN THE COVE

THE first three days at Tremannon Farm were lazy, uneventful days, full of sunshine, good food, dogs – and of little Yan.

He really was a perfect nuisance. The four children seemed to have a real fascination for him, and he trailed them everywhere, following them bare-footed. He turned up behind hedges, along lanes, at their picnicking places, his dark eyes watching them intently.

'What's the good of telling him to go?' groaned Julian. 'He disappears behind one hedge and appears out of another. You'd think he'd get bored, doing this shadowing business all the time. What's the point of it, anyway?'

'No point,' said George. 'Just curiosity. What I can't understand is why Timmy puts up with him. You'd think he'd bark or growl or something, but he's quite silly with Yan, lets him play with him, and roll him over as if he was a mad puppy.'

'Well, I'm going to find this Great-Grandad of his tomorrow, and tell him to keep Yan with him,' said Julian. 'He's maddening. I feel I want to swot him

like a gnat, always buzzing round us. Gosh, there he
is again!'

So he was. A pair of dark eyes were gazing round a
tree-trunk, half hidden by a sheaf of leaves. Timmy
bounded up to him in glee, and made such a fuss of
Yan that George was quite disgusted.

'Timmy! Come here!' she called, imperiously.
'Don't you understand that you ought to chase Yan
away when he comes and not encourage him? I'm
ashamed of you!'

Timmy put his tail down and went to her. He sat
down beside her with a bump. Dick laughed.

'He's sulking! He won't look at you, George! He's
turning his head away on purpose!'

Julian chased Yan away, threatening him with all
sorts of things if he caught him, but the boy was as
fast as a hare, and seemed suddenly to disappear into
thin air. He had a wonderful way of vanishing, and an
equally remarkable way of appearing again.

'I don't like that kid,' said Julian. 'He makes me
shiver down my back whenever I see him suddenly
peeping somewhere.'

'He can't be a bad kid, though, because Timmy likes
him so much,' said Anne, who had great faith in
Timmy's judgement. 'Timmy never likes anyone horrid.'

'Well, he's made a mistake this time, then,' said
George, who was cross with Timmy. 'He's being very
stupid. I'm not pleased with you, Timmy!'

'Let's go down to the sea and bathe,' said Dick.

'We'll go on our bikes and Yan won't be able to pop up and watch us there.'

They took their bicycles and rode off to the coast. Mrs Penruthlan made them sandwiches and gave them fruit cake and drinks to take with them. They saw Yan watching them from behind a hedge as they went.

They took the road to the sea. It was no more than a narrow lane, and wound about like a stream, twisting and turning so that they couldn't get up any speed at all.

'Look – the sea!' cried Dick, as they rounded one last bend. The lane had run down between two high, rocky cliffs, and in front of them was a cove into which raced enormous breakers, throwing spray high into the air.

They left their bicycles at the top of the cove, and went behind some big rocks to change into bathing things. When they came out, Julian looked at the sea. It was calm beyond the rocks, but over these the waters raged fiercely and it was impossible to venture in.

They walked a little way round the cliffs, and came to a great pool lying in a rocky hollow. 'Just the thing!' cried George and plunged in. 'Gosh, it's cold!'

It should have been hot from the sun, but every now and again an extra large wave broke right into the pool itself, bringing in cooler water. It was fun when that happened. The four of them swam to their hearts' content, and Timmy had a fine time too.

They picnicked on the rocks, with spray flying round them, and then went to explore round the foot of the cliffs.

'This is exciting,' said George. 'Caves, and more caves, and yet more caves! And cove after cove, all as lovely as the one before. I suppose when the tide's in, all these coves are shoulder-high in water.'

'My word, yes,' said Julian, who was keeping a very sharp eye indeed on the tide. 'And a good many of these caves would be flooded too. No wonder Mrs Penruthlan warned us so solemnly about the tides here! I wouldn't want to try and climb up these cliffs if we were caught!'

Anne looked up and shivered. They were so very steep and high. They frowned down at her as if to say 'We stand no nonsense from anyone! So look after yourself!'

'Well, I'm blessed! Look there, isn't that that tiresome little wretch of a Yan?' said Dick, suddenly. He pointed to a rock covered with seaweed. Peeping from behind it was Yan!

'He must have run all the way here, and found us,' said Julian in disgust. 'Well, we'll leave him here. It's time we went. The tide's coming in. It'll serve him right to find us gone as soon as he arrives. He must be mad!'

'Do you think he knows about the tide?' said Anne, looking worried. 'I mean, knows that it's coming in and might catch him?'

'Of course he knows!' said Julian. 'Don't be silly.

But we'll wait and have our tea at the top part of the cove, if you like. That's the only way back, if he wants to escape the tide, short of climbing the cliff, which no one would be mad enough to try!'

They had put aside some cake and biscuits for their tea, and they found a good picnicking place at the top of the cove where they had left their bicycles. They settled down to munch the solid fruit cake that Mrs Penruthlan had given them. There was no doubt about it, she was a wonderful cook!

The tide swept in at a great rate, and soon the noise of enormous waves pounding on the rocks grew louder. 'Yan hasn't appeared yet,' said Anne. 'Do you think he's all right?'

'He must be having a good old wetting if he's still there,' said Dick. 'I think we'd better go and see. Much as I dislike him I don't want him to be drowned.'

The two boys went down the cove as far as they could, peering round the cliff to where they had seen Yan hiding. But how different it all looked now!

'Gosh, the beach is gone already!' said Julian, startled. 'I can see how easily anyone could get caught by the tide now, see that last wave, it swept right into that cave we explored!'

'What's happened to Yan?' said Dick. 'He's nowhere to be seen. He didn't come out of the cove; we've been sitting there all the time. Where is he?'

Dick spoke urgently, and Julian began to feel scared too. He hesitated. Should they wade over the rocks a little way? The next wave decided him. It would be

folly to do any such thing! Another wave like that and
both he and Dick would be flung off the rock they
were standing on!

'Look out, here comes an even bigger one!' yelled
Julian, and the two boys leapt off their rock and raced
back up the cove. Even so, the wave lapped right up
to their feet.

They went back to the girls. 'Can't see him anywhere,' said Julian, speaking more cheerfully than he
felt. 'The whole beach is covered with the tide now,
more than covered. The lower caves are full too.'

'He – he won't be drowned, will he?' said Anne,
fearfully.

'Oh, I expect he can look after himself,' said Julian.
'He's used to this coast. Come on, it's time we went.'

They all rode off, Timmy running beside their
bicycles. Nobody said anything. They couldn't help
feeling worried about Yan. Whatever could have happened to him?

They arrived at the farm and put their bicycles
away. They went in to find Mrs Penruthlan. They
told her about Yan, and how he had disappeared.

'You don't think he might have been swept off his
feet and drowned, do you?' asked Anne.

Mrs Penruthlan laughed. 'Good gracious, no! That
boy knows his way about the countryside and the sea-
shore blindfold. He's cleverer than you think. He never
misses anything! He's a poor little thing, but he looks
after himself all right!'

This was rather comforting. Perhaps Yan would

turn up again, with his dark eyes fixed unblinkingly
on them!

After a high-tea as good as any they had had, they
went for a walk down the honeysuckle-scented lanes,
accompanied as usual by the five dogs. They sat on a
stile, and Dick handed round some barley-sugar.

'Look!' said George suddenly. 'Do you see what I
see? Look!' She nodded her head towards an oak tree
in the hedge, not far off. The others stared up into it.

Two dark eyes stared back. Yan! He had followed
them as usual, and had hidden himself to watch them.
Anne was so tremendously relieved to see him that she
called to him in delight.

'Oh, Yan! Have a barley-sugar?'

Yan slithered down the tree at top speed and came
up. He held out his hand for the barley-sugar. For the
first time he smiled, and his dirty, sullen face lighted
up enchantingly. Anne stared at him. Why, he was a
dear little fellow! His eyes shone and twinkled, and a
dimple came in each cheek.

'Here you are, here's a couple more sweets for you,'
Dick said, very glad to see that the small boy hadn't
been drowned. Yan almost snatched them from him!
It was plain that he very, very seldom had any sweets!
Timmy was making a fuss of him as usual. He lay
down on his back and rolled over Yan's feet. He licked
his fingers, and jumped up at him, almost knocking
the boy down. Yan laughed, and fell on Timmy, rolling over and over with him. Julian, Dick and Anne
watched and laughed.

But George was not pleased. Timmy was her dog, and she didn't like him to make a fuss of anyone she disapproved of. She was glad that Yan was safe but she still didn't like him! So she scowled, and Julian nudged Dick to make him see the scowl. George saw him and scowled worse than ever.

'You'll be sorry you gave him sweets,' she said. 'He'll be round us worse than ever now.'

Yan came up after a minute or two, sucking all

three sweets at once, so that his right cheek was very swollen indeed.

'Come, see my Grandad,' he said, earnestly, talking even worse than usual because of the sweets. 'I tell him 'bout you all. He tell you many things.'

He stared at them all seriously. 'Grandad likes sweets too,' he added, solemnly. 'Iss. Iss, he do.'

Julian laughed. 'All right. We'll come and see him tomorrow afternoon. Now you clear off or you won't get any more sweets. Understand?'

'Iss,' said Yan, nodding his head. He took the three sweets out of his mouth, looked at them to see how much he had sucked them, and then put them back again.

'Clear off now,' said Julian again. 'But wait a bit, I've just thought; how did you get away from that beach this afternoon? Did you climb that cliff?'

'No,' said Yan, shifting his sweets to the other cheek. 'I came the Wreckers' Way. My Grandad learnt it me.'

He was off and away before anyone could ask him another question. The four looked at one another. 'Did you hear that?' said Julian. 'He went the Wreckers' Way. What's that, do you suppose? We must have been on one of the beaches the wreckers used long, long ago.'

'Yes. But how did he get off that beach, and away into safety?' said Dick. 'I'd like to know more about the Wreckers' Way! I certainly think we'd better pay a visit to old Great-Grandad tomorrow. He might have some very interesting things to tell us.'

'Well, we'll go and see him,' said George, getting up. 'But just you remember what I said. Yan will pester us more than ever now we've encouraged him.'

'Oh well, he doesn't seem such a bad kid after all,' said Dick, remembering that sudden smile and the eager acceptance of a few sweets. 'And if he persuades Grandad to let us into the secret of Wreckers' Way, we might have some fun doing a bit of exploring. Don't you think so, Ju?'

'It might even lead to an adventure,' said Julian, laughing at Anne's serious face. 'Cheer up, Anne. I can't even *smell* an adventure in Tremannon. I'm just pulling your leg!'

'I think you're wrong,' said Anne. 'If *you* can't smell one somewhere, I can. I don't want to, but I can!'

Chapter Five

YAN – AND HIS GRANDAD

THE next day was Sunday. It made no difference to
the time that the two Penruthlans got up, however. As
Mrs Penruthlan said, the cows and horses, hens and
ducks didn't approve of late Sunday breakfasts! They
wanted attending to at exactly the same time each
day!

'Will you be going to church?' asked Mrs Penruthlan. 'It's a beautiful walk across the fields to Tremannon Church, and you'd like Parson. He's a good man,
he is.'

'Yes, we're all going,' said Julian. 'We can tie Timmy
up outside. He's used to that. And we thought we'd
go up and see your old shepherd this afternoon, Mrs
Penruthlan, and see what tales he has to tell.'

'Yan will show you the way,' said the farmer's wife,
bustling off to her cooking. 'I'll get you a fine Sunday
dinner. Do you like fresh fruit salad with cream?'

'Rather!' said everyone at once.

'Can't we help you to do something?' said Anne.
'I've just seen all the peas you're going to shell. Piles
of them! And don't you want help with those red

currants? I love getting the currants off their stalks
with a fork!'

'Well, you'll have a few odd minutes before you go
to church, I expect,' said Mrs Penruthlan, looking
pleased. 'It *would* be a bit of help today. But the boys
needn't help.'

'I like that!' said George, indignantly. 'How un-
fair! Why shouldn't they, just because they're boys?'

'Don't fly off the handle, George,' grinned Dick.
'We're going to help, don't worry. We like podding
peas too! You're not going to have all the treats!'

Dick had a very neat way of turning the tables on
George when he saw her flying into a tantrum. She
smiled unwillingly. She was always jealous of the boys
because she so badly wanted to be one herself, and
wasn't! She hitched up her jeans, and went to get a
pan of peas to shell.

Soon the noise of the popping of pods was to be
heard, a very pleasant noise, Anne thought. The four
of them sat on the big kitchen step, out in the sun, with
Timmy sitting beside them, watching with interest. He
didn't stay with them long though.

Up came his four friends, the little Scottie trotting
valiantly behind, trying to keep up with the longer
legs of the others. 'Woof!' said the biggest collie.
Timmy wagged his tail politely, but didn't stir.

'Woof!' said the collie again, and pranced around
invitingly.

'Timmy! He says "Will you come and play?"' said
George. 'Aren't you going? You aren't the least help

with shelling peas, and you keep breathing down my neck.'

Timmy gave George a flying lick and leapt off the step joyfully. He pounced on the Scottie, rolled him over, and then took on all three collies at once. They were big, strong dogs, but no match for Timmy!

'Look at him,' said George, proudly. 'He can manage the whole lot single-handed.'

'Single-footed!' said Dick. 'He's faster than even that biggest collie and stronger than the whole lot. Good old Tim. He's come in jolly useful in some of our adventures!'

'I've no doubt he will again,' said Julian. 'I'd rather have one Timmy than two police-dogs.'

'I should think his ears are burning, the way we're talking about him!' said Anne. 'Oh, sorry, Dick, that pod popped unexpectedly!'

'That's the second lot of peas you've shot all over me,' said Dick, scrabbling inside his shirt. 'I *must* just find one that went down my neck, or I shall be fidgeting all through church.'

'You always do,' said Anne. 'Look – isn't that Yan?'

It was! He came sidling up, looking as dirty as ever, and gave them a quick smile that once more entirely changed his sullen little face. He held out his hand, palm upwards, and said something.

'What's he saying?' said Dick. 'Oh, he's asking for a sweet.'

'Don't give him one,' said Julian, quickly. 'Don't turn him into a little beggar. Make him *work* for a sweet this time. Yan, if you want a sweet, you can help pod these peas.'

Mrs Penruthlan appeared at once. 'But see he washes those filthy hands first,' she commanded, and disappeared again. Yan looked at his hands, then put them under his arm-pits.

'Go and wash them,' said Julian. But Yan shook his head, and sat down a little way away from them.

'All right. Don't wash your hands. Don't shell the peas. Don't have a sweet,' said George.

Yan scowled at George. He didn't seem to like her any more than she liked him. He waited till someone split a pod, and a few peas shot out on to the ground instead of into the dish. Then he darted at them, picked them up and ate them. He was as quick as a cat.

'My Grandad says come see him,' announced Yan. 'I take you.'

'Right,' said Julian. 'We'll come this afternoon. We'll get Mrs Penruthlan to pack us up a basket, and we'll have tea in the hills. You can share it if you wash your hands and face.'

'I shouldn't think he's ever washed himself in his life,' said George. 'Oh, here's Timmy come back. I will *not* have him fawn round that dirty little boy. Here, Timmy!'

But Timmy darted to Yan with the greatest delight and pawed at him to come and have a game. They began to roll over and over like two puppies.

'If you're going to church, you'd better get ready,'

said Mrs Penruthlan, appearing again, this time with arms floured up to the elbow. 'My, what a lot of peas you've done for me!'

'I wish I had time to do the red currants,' said Anne. 'We've practically finished the peas, anyway, Mrs Penruthlan. We've done thousands, I should think!'

'Ah, Mr Penruthlan is real fond of peas,' said the farmer's wife. 'He can eat a whole tureen at one sitting.'

She disappeared again. The children went to get ready for church, and then off they went. It certainly was a lovely walk over the fields, with honeysuckle trailing everywhere!

The church was small and old and lovely. Yan went with them, trailing behind, right to the church door. When he saw George tying Timmy up to a railing, he sat down beside him and looked pleased. George didn't look pleased, however. Now Timmy and Yan would play about together all the time she was in church! How annoying!

The church was cool and dark, except for three lovely stained-glass windows through which the sun poured, its brilliance dimmed by the colours of the glass. 'Parson' was as nice as Mrs Penruthlan had said, a simple, friendly person whose words were listened to by everyone, from an old, old woman bent almost double in a corner to a solemn-eyed five year old clutching her mother's hand.

It was dazzling to come out into the sun again from the cool dimness of the church. Timmy barked a wel-

come. Yan was still there, sitting with his arm round
Timmy's neck. He gave them his sudden smile, and
untied Timmy, who promptly went mad and tore out
of the churchyard at sixty miles an hour. He always
did that when he had been tied up.

'You come see Grandad,' said Yan to Dick, and
pulled at his arm.

'This afternoon,' said Dick. 'You can show us the
way. Come after dinner.'

So, after the children had had a dinner of cold
boiled beef and carrots, with a dumpling each, and
'lashings' of peas and new potatoes, followed by a
truly magnificent fruit salad and cream, Yan appeared
at the door to take them to his Grandad.

'Did you see the amount of peas that Mr Penruthlan
got through?' said Anne, in awe. 'I should think he
really *did* manage a tureen all to himself. I wish he'd
say something beside "Ah" and "Ock" and the other
peculiar sounds he makes. Conversation is awfully
difficult with him.'

'Is Yan taking you up to Grandad?' called Mrs
Penruthlan. 'I'll put a few cakes in the basket for him,
too, then, and for Grandad.'

'*Don't* put us up a big tea,' begged Dick. 'We only
want a snack, just to keep us going till high-tea.'

But all the same the basket was quite heavy when
Mrs Penruthlan had finished packing it!

It was a long walk over the fields to the shepherd's
hut. Yan led the way proudly. They crossed the fields,
and climbed stiles, walked up narrow cart-paths, and

at last came to a cone-shaped hill on which sheep grazed peacefully. Half-grown lambs, wearing their woolly coats, unlike the shorn sheep, gambolled here and there – then remembered that they were nearly grown up, and walked sedately.

The old shepherd was sitting outside his hut, smoking a clay pipe. He wasn't very big, and he seemed shrivelled up, like an apple stored too long. But there was still sweetness in him, and the children liked him at once. He had Yan's sudden smile, that lighted up eyes that were still as blue as the summer sky above.

His face had a thousand wrinkles that creased and ran into one another when he smiled. His shaggy eyebrows, curly beard and hair were all grey, as grey as the woolly coats of the sheep he had lived with all his life.

'You be welcome,' he said, in his slow Cornish voice. 'Yan here have told me about you.'

'We've brought our tea to share with you,' said Dick. 'We'll have it later on. Is it true that your father was one of the Wreckers in the old days?'

The old fellow nodded his head. Julian got out a bag of boiled sweets, and offered them to the old man. He took one eagerly. Yan edged up at once and was given one too.

Judging by the crunching that went on old Grandad still had plenty of teeth! When the sweet had gone, he began to talk. He talked slowly and simply, almost as Yan might have done, and sometimes paused to find a word he wanted.

Living with sheep all his life doesn't make for easy talking, thought Julian, interested in this old man with the wise, keen eyes. He must be much more at home with sheep than with human beings.

Grandad certainly had some interesting things to tell them, dreadful things, Anne thought.

'You've seen them rocks down on Tremannon coast,' began Grandad. 'Wicked rocks they be, hungry for ships and men. There's many a ship been wrecked on purpose! Ay, you can look disbelieving-like, but it's true.'

'How did they get wrecked on purpose?' asked Dick. 'Were they lured here by a false light, or something?'

The old man lowered his voice as if he was afraid of being overheard.

'Way back up the coast, more than a hundred years ago, there was a light set to guide the ships that sail round here,' said Grandad. 'They were to sail towards that light, and then hug the coast and avoid the rocks that stood out to sea. They were safe then. But, on wild nights, a light was set two miles farther down the coast, to bemuse lost ships, and drag them to the rocks round Tremannon coves.'

'How wicked!' said Anne and George together. 'How *could* men do that?'

'It's fair amazing what men will do,' said Grandad, nodding his head. 'Take my old Dad now – a kind man he was and went to church, so he did, and took me with him. But he was the one that set the false light burning every time, and sent men to watch the ship

coming in on the rocks – crashing over them to break
into pieces.'

'Did you – did you ever see a ship crashing to its
death?' asked Dick, imagining the groaning of the
sailing ships, and the groaning of the men flung into
the raging sea.

'Ay. I did so,' said Grandad, his eyes taking on a
very far-away look. 'I were sent to the cove with the
men, and had to hold a lantern to bemuse the ship
again when she came to the rocks. Poor thing, she
groaned like a live thing, she did, when she ran into
them wicked rocks, and split into pieces. And next day
I went to the cove to help get the goods that were
scattered all around the cove. There were lots drown-
ded that night, and . . .'

'Don't tell us about that,' said Dick, feeling sick.
'Where did they flash the false light from? From these
hills, or from the cliff somewhere?'

'I'll show you where my Dad flashed it from,' said
Grandad, and he got up slowly. 'There's only one
place on these hills where you could see the light a-
flashing. The wreckers had to find somewhere well
hidden, so that their wicked light couldn't be seen
from inland, or the police would stop it, but it could be
seen plainly by any ship on the sea near this coast!'

He took them round his hill, and then pointed towards the coast. Set between two hills there the roof
of a house could just be seen, and from it rose a tower.
It could only be seen from that one spot! Dick took a
few steps to each side of it, and at once the house dis-

appeared behind one or other of the hills on each side of it.

'I were the only one that ever knew the false light could be seen from inland,' said Grandad, pointing with his pipe-stem towards the far-off square tower. 'I were watching lambs one night up here, and I saw the light a-flashing. And I heard there was a ship wrecked down in Tremannon cove that night so I reckoned it were the wreckers at work.'

'Did you often see the light flashing over there, when you watched the sheep?' asked George.

'Oh ay, many a time,' said the shepherd. 'And always on wild, stormy nights, when ships were labouring along, and in trouble, looking for some light to guide them into shore. Then a light would flare out over there, and I'd say to meself "Now may the Good God help those sailors tonight, for it's sure that nobody else will!"'

'How horrible!' said George, quite appalled at such wickedness. 'You must be glad that you never see that false light shining there on stormy nights now!'

Grandad looked at George, and his eyes were scared and strange. He lowered his voice and spoke to George as if she were a boy.

'Little master,' he said, 'that light still flares on dark and stormy nights. The place is a ruin, and jackdaws build in the tower. But three times this year I've seen that light again! Come a stormy night it'll flare again! I know it in my bones, little master, I know it in my bones!'

Chapter Six

A QUEER TALE

THE four children shivered suddenly in the hot sun, as they listened to the shepherd's strange words. Were they true? Did the wreckers' light still flash in the old tower on wild and stormy nights? But why should it? Surely no wreckers any longer did their dreadful work on this lonely rocky coast?

Dick voiced the thoughts of the others. 'But surely there are no wrecks on this coast now? Isn't there a good lighthouse farther up, to warn ships to keep right out to sea?'

Grandad nodded his grey head. 'Yes. There's a lighthouse, and there's not been a wreck along this coast for more years than I can remember. But I tell you that light flares up just as it used to do. I seen it with my own eyes, and there's nought wrong with them yet!'

'I seen it too,' put in Yan, suddenly.

Grandad looked at Yan, annoyed. 'You hold your noise, you,' he commanded. 'You've never seen no light. You sleeps like a babe at nights.'

'I seen it,' said Yan, obstinately, and moved out of

Grandad's way quickly as the old man raised his hand
to cuff the small boy.

Dick changed the subject. 'Grandad, do you know
anything about the Wreckers' Way?' he asked. 'Is it a
secret way to get down to the coves from inland? Was
it used by the wreckers?'

Grandad frowned. 'That be a secret,' he said,
shortly. 'My Dad, he showed it to me, and I swore as
I never would tell. Us all had to swear and promise
that.'

'But Yan here said that you taught the way to him,'
said Dick, puzzled.

Yan promptly removed himself from the company
and disappeared round a clump of bushes. His old
Great-Grandad glared round at the disappearing boy.

'Yan! That boy! He doesn't know anything about
the Wreckers' Way. It's lost and forgotten by every
man living. I'm the last one left as knows of it. Yan!
He's dreaming! Maybe he's heard *tell* of an old
Wreckers' Way, but that's all.'

'Oh!' said Dick, disappointed. He had hoped that
Grandad would tell them the old way, and then they
could go and explore it. Perhaps they could go and
search for it, anyhow! It would be fun to do that.

Julian came back to the question of the light flashing
from the old tower by the coast. He was puzzled. 'Who
could possibly flash that light?' he said to Grandad.
'You say the place is a ruin. Are you sure it wasn't
lightning you saw? You said it came on a wild and
stormy night.'

'It weren't lightning,' said the old man shortly. 'I first saw that light near ninety years ago, and I tell you I saw it again three times this year, same place, same light, same weather! And if you told me it weren't flashed by mortal hands, I'd believe you.'

There was a silence after this extraordinary statement. Anne looked over towards the far-off tower that showed just between the two distant hills. How queer that this spot where they were standing was the only place from which the tower could be seen from inland. The wreckers had been clever to choose a spot like that to flash a light from. No one but old Grandad up on the hills could possibly have seen the light and guessed what was going on, no one but the callous wreckers themselves.

Grandad delved deep into more memories stored in his mind. He poured them out, tales of the old days, queer, unbelievable stories. One was about an old woman who was said to be a witch. The things she did!

The four stared at the old shepherd, marvelling to think they were, in a way, linked with the witches and brownies, the wreckers and the killers of long-ago days, through this old, old man.

Yan appeared again as soon as Julian opened the tea-basket. They had now gone back to the hut, and sat outside in the sunshine, surrounded by nibbling sheep. One or two of the half-grown lambs came up, looking hot in their unshorn woolly coats. They nosed round the old shepherd, and he rubbed their woolly noses.

'These be lambs I fed from a bottle,' he explained. 'They always remember. Go away now, Woolly. Cake's wasted on you.'

Yan wolfed quite half the tea. He gave Anne a quick grin of pure pleasure, showing both his dimples at once. She smiled back. She liked this funny little boy now, and felt sorry for him. She was sure that his old Grandad didn't give him enough to eat!

The church bells began to ring, and the sun was now sliding down the sky. 'We must go,' said Julian, reluctantly. 'It's quite a long walk back. Thanks for a most interesting afternoon, Grandad. I expect you'll be glad to be rid of us now, and smoke your pipe in peace with your sheep around you.'

'Ay, I will,' said Grandad, truthfully. 'I do be one for my own company, and I likes to think my own thoughts. Long thoughts they be, too, going back nigh on a hundred years. If I wants to talk, I talks to my sheep. It's rare and wunnerful how they listen.'

The children laughed, but Grandad was quite solemn, and meant every word he said. They packed up the basket, and said good-bye to the old man.

'Well, what do you think he meant when he talked about the light still flashing in the old tower?' said Dick, as they went over the hills back to the farm. 'What an extraordinary thing to say. Was it true, do you suppose?'

'There's only one way to find out!' said George, her eyes dancing. 'Wait for a wild and stormy night and go and see!'

'But what about our agreement?' said Julian, solemnly. 'If anything exciting seems about to happen we turn our backs on it. That's what we decided. Don't you remember?'

'Pooh!' said George.

'We ought to keep the agreement,' said Anne, doubtfully. She knew quite well that the others didn't think so!

'Look! Who are all these people?' said Dick, suddenly. They were just climbing over a stile to cross a lane to another field.

They sat on the stile and stared. Some carts were going by, open wagons, their canvas tops folded down. They were the most old-fashioned carts the children had ever seen, not in the least like gipsy caravans.

Ten or eleven people were with the wagons, dressed in the clothes of other days! Some rode in the wagons and some walked. Some were middle-aged, some were young, but they all looked cheerful and gay.

The children stared. After Grandad's tales of long ago these old-time folk seemed just right! For a few moments Anne felt herself back in Grandad's time, when he was a boy. He must have seen people dressed like these!

'Who are they?' she said, wonderingly. And then the children saw red lettering painted on the biggest cart:

THE BARNIES

'Oh! It's the Barnies! Don't you remember Mrs Penruthlan telling us about them?' said Anne. 'The strolling players, who play to the country folk around, in the barns. What fun!'

The Barnies waved to the watching children. One man, dressed in velvet and lace, with a sword at his side, and a wig of curly hair, threw a leaflet or two to them. They read them with interest.

THE BARNIES ARE COMING!

They will sing, they will dance, they will fiddle.
They will perform plays of all kinds.
Edith Wells, the nightingale singer.
Bonnie Carter, the old-time dancer.
Janie Coster and her fiddle.
John Walters, finest tenor in the world.
George Roth – he'll make you laugh!
And Others.
We also present Clopper, the Funniest Horse in the
World!

THE BARNIES ARE COMING!

'This'll be fun!' said George, pleased. She called out to the passing wagons: 'Will you be playing at Tremannon Farm?'

'Oh, yes!' called a man with bright, merry eyes. 'We always play there. You staying there?'

'Yes,' said George. 'We'll look out for you all. Where are you going now?'

'To Poltelly Farm for the night,' called the man. 'We'll be at Tremannon soon.'

The wagons passed, and the gay, queerly-dressed

players went out of sight. 'Good,' said Dick. 'Their show may not be first-rate, but it's sure to be funny. They looked a merry lot.'

'All but the man driving the front cart. Did you see him?' said Anne. 'He looked pretty grim, I thought.'

Nobody else had noticed him. 'He was probably the owner of the Barnies,' said Dick. 'And has got all the organisation on his shoulders. Well, come on. Where's Timmy?'

They looked round for him, and George frowned. Yan had followed them as usual, and Timmy was playing with him. Bother Yan! Was he going to trail them all day and every day?

They went back to the peaceful farm-house. Hens were still clucking around and ducks were quacking. A horse stamped somewhere near by, and the grunting of pigs came on the air. It all looked quite perfect.

Footsteps came through the farm-yard, and Mr Penruthlan came by. He grunted at them and went into a barn.

Anne spoke in almost a whisper. 'I can imagine *him* living in the olden days and being a wrecker. I can really!'

'Yes! I know what you mean,' said Dick. 'He's so fierce-looking and determined. What's the word I want? *Ruthless!* I'm sure he would have made a good wrecker!'

'Do you suppose there *are* any wreckers now, and that light really *is* flashed to make ships go on the rocks?' said George.

'Well, I shouldn't have thought there were any wreckers in *this* country, anyway,' said Dick. 'I can't imagine that such a thing would be tolerated for an instant. But if that light *is* flashed, what is it flashed for?'

'Old Grandad said there hadn't been any wrecks on this coast for ages,' said Julian. 'I think really that the old man is wandering a bit in his mind about that light!'

'But Yan said he had seen it, too,' said Anne.

'I'm not sure that Yan's as truthful as he might be!' said Julian.

'Why did Grandad say that the light isn't flashed by mortal hands now?' asked George. 'It must be! I can't imagine any other hands working it! He surely doesn't think that his father is still doing it?'

There was a pause. 'We could easily find out if we popped over to that tower and had a look at it,' said Dick.

There was another pause. 'I thought we said we wouldn't go poking about in anything mysterious,' said Anne.

'This isn't really mysterious,' argued Dick. 'It's just a story an old man remembers, and I really *can't* believe that that light still flashes on a wild stormy night. Grandad must have seen lightning or something. Why don't we settle the matter for good and all and go and explore the old house with the tower?'

'I should like to,' said George firmly. 'I never was keen on this "Keep away from anything unusual" idea we suddenly had. We've got Timmy with us – we can't possibly come to any harm!'

'All right,' said Anne, with a sigh. 'I give up. We'll go if you want to.'

'Good old Anne,' said Dick, giving her a friendly slap on the back. 'But *you* needn't come, you know. Why don't you stay behind and hear our story when we come back?'

'Certainly *not*,' said Anne, quite cross. 'I may not want to go as much as you do, but I'm not going to be left out of anything, so don't think it!'

'All right. It's settled then,' said Julian. 'We take our opportunity and go as soon as we can. Tomorrow, perhaps.'

Mrs Penruthlan came to the door and called them. 'Your high tea is ready. You must be hungry. Come along indoors.'

The sun suddenly went in. Julian looked up at the sky in surprise. 'My word, look at those black clouds!' he said. 'There's a storm coming! Well, I thought there might be, it's been so terribly hot all day!'

'A storm!' said George. 'That light flashes on wild and stormy nights! Oh, Julian, do you think it will flash tonight? Can't we – *can't* we go and see?'

Chapter Seven

OUT IN THE NIGHT

BEFORE the children had finished their high tea, the big kitchen-sitting-room was quite dark. Thunder clouds had moved up from the west, gathering together silently, frowning and sinister. Then, from far off, came the first rumble of thunder.

The little Scottie came and cowered against Mrs Penruthlan's skirts. He hated storms. The farmer's wife comforted him, and her big husband gave a little unexpected snort of laughter. He said something that sounded like 'oose'.

'He's *not* as timid as a mouse,' said his wife, who was really marvellous at interpreting her husband's peculiar noises. 'He just doesn't like the thunder. He never did. He can sleep with us in our room tonight.'

There were a few more sounds from Mr Penruthlan to which his wife listened anxiously. 'Very well, if you have to get up and see to Jenny the horse in the night, I'll see Benny doesn't bark the house down,' she said. She turned to the children. 'Don't worry if you hear him barking,' she said. 'It will only be Mr Penruthlan stirring.'

The thunder crashed and rumbled again, this time

a little nearer, and then lightning flashed. Then down came the rain. How it poured! It rattled and clattered on the roof in enormous drops, and then settled down into a steady downpour.

The four children got out their cards and played games by the light of the oil lamp. There was no electricity at Tremannon. Timmy sat with his head on George's knee. He didn't mind the thunder but he didn't particularly like it.

'Well, I think we'd better go to bed,' said Julian at

last. He knew that the Penruthlans liked to go to bed early because they got up so early, and as they did not go upstairs until after the children did, Julian saw to it that they, too, went early.

They said good night and went up to their bare little rooms. The windows were still open and the small curtains drawn back, so that the hills, lit now and again by lightning, showed up clearly. The children went and stood there, watching. They all loved a storm, especially Dick. There was something powerful and most majestic about this kind of storm, sweeping over hills and sea, rumbling all round, and tearing the sky in half with flashes of lightning.

'Julian, is it possible to go up to that place the shepherd showed us and see if the light flashes tonight?' said George. 'You only laughed when I asked you before.'

'Well, I laugh again!' said Julian. 'Of course not! We'd be drenched, and I don't fancy being out in this lightning on those exposed hills, either.'

'All right,' said George. 'Anyway, I don't feel *quite* such an urge to go now that it's so pitch dark.'

'Just as well,' said Julian. 'Come on, Dick, let's go to bed.'

The storm went on for some time, rumbling all round the hills again, as if it were going round in a circle. The girls fell asleep, but the boys tossed about, feeling hot and sticky.

'Dick,' said Julian, suddenly, 'let's get up and go out. It's stopped raining. Let's go and see if that light is flashing tonight. It should be just the night for it, according to old Grandad.'

'Right,' said Dick, and sat up, feeling for his clothes. 'I simply can't go to sleep, even though I felt really sleepy when I undressed.'

They pulled on as few clothes as possible, for the night was still thundery and hot. Julian took his torch and Dick hunted for his.

'Got it,' he said at last. 'Are you ready? Come on, then. Let's tiptoe past the Penruthlans' door, or we may wake that Scottie dog ! He's sleeping there to-night, don't forget.'

They tiptoed along the passage, past the Penruth-lans' door and down the stairs. One stair creaked rather alarmingly, and they stopped in dismay, wondering if Ben the Scottie would break out into a storm of barking.

But he didn't. Good! Down they went again, switching on their torches to see the way. They came to the bottom of the stairs. 'Shall we go out by the front door or back door, Ju?' whispered Dick.

'Back,' said Julian. 'The front door's so heavy to open. Come on.'

So they went down the passage to the back door that led out from the kitchen. It was locked and bolted, but the two boys opened it without too much noise.

They stepped out into the night. The rain had now stopped, but the sky was still dark and overclouded. The thunder rumbled away in the distance. A wind had got up and blew coolly against the boys' faces.

'Nice cool breeze,' whispered Dick. 'Now – do we go through the farm-yard? Is that the shortest way to the stile we have to climb over into that first field?'

'Yes, I think so,' said Julian. They made their way across the silent farm-yard, where, in the daytime, such a lot of noise went on, clucking, quacking, grunting, clip-clopping, and shouting!

Now it was dark and deserted. They passed the barns and the stables. A little 'hrrrrrumphing' came from one of the stables. 'That's Jenny, the horse that's not well,' said Julian, stopping. 'Let's just have a look at her and see if she's all right. She was lying down feeling very sorry for herself when I saw her last.'

They flashed their torch over the top half of the stable door, which was pulled back to let in air. They looked in with interest.

Jenny was no longer lying down. She was standing up, munching something. Goodness, she must be quite all right again! She whinnied to the two boys.

They left her and went on. They came to the stile and climbed over. The rain began drizzling again, and if the boys had not had their torches with them they would not have been able to see a step in front of them, it was so dark.

'I say, Ju – did you hear that?' said Dick, stopping suddenly.

'No. What?' said Julian, listening.

'Well, it sounded like a cough,' said Dick.

'One of the sheep,' suggested Julian. 'I heard one old sheep coughing just like Uncle Quentin does sometimes, sort of hollow and mournful.'

'No. It wasn't a sheep,' said Dick. 'Anyway, there aren't any in this field.'

'You imagined it,' said Julian. 'I bet there's nobody idiotic enough to be out on a night like this, except ourselves!'

They went on cautiously over the field. The thunder began again, a little nearer. Then came a flash, and again the thunder. Dick stopped dead once more and clutched Julian's arm.

'There's somebody a good way in front of us, the lightning just lighted him up for half a second. He was climbing over that stile, the one we're making for. Who do you suppose it is on a night like this?'

'He's apparently going the same way that we are,' said Julian. 'Well, I suppose if we saw *him* he's quite likely to have seen *us*!'

'Not unless he was looking backwards,' said Dick. 'Come on, let's see where he's going.'

They went on cautiously towards the stile. They came to it and climbed over. And then a hand suddenly clutched hold of Dick's shoulder!

He jumped almost out of his skin! The hand gripped him so hard and so fiercely that Dick shouted in pain and tried to wriggle away from the powerful grip.

Julian felt a hand lunge at him, too, but dodged and pressed himself into the hedge. He switched off his torch at once and stood quite still, his heart thumping.

'Let me go!' shouted Dick, wriggling like an eel. His shirt was almost torn off his back in his struggles. He kicked out at the man's ankles and for one moment his captor loosened his grasp. That was enough for Dick. He ripped himself away and left his shirt in the man's hand!

He ran up the lane into which the stile had led and flung himself under a bush in the darkness, panting. He heard his captor coming along, muttering, and Dick pressed himself farther into the bush. A torchlight swept the ground near him, but missed him.

Dick waited till the footsteps had gone and then

crawled out. He went quietly down the lane. 'Julian!'
he whispered, and jumped as a voice answered almost
in his ear, just above his head!

'I'm here. Are you all right?'

Dick looked up into the darkness of a tree, but could
see nothing. 'I've dropped my torch somewhere,' he
said. 'Where are you, Ju? Up in the tree?'

A hand groped out and felt his head. 'Here I am, on
the first branch,' said Julian. 'I hid in the hedge first
and then climbed up here. I daren't put on my torch
in case that fellow's anywhere around and sees it.'

'He's gone up the lane,' said Dick. 'My word, he
nearly wrenched my shoulder off. Half my shirt's
gone! Who was he? Did you see?'

'No, I didn't,' said Julian, clambering down. 'Let's
find your torch before we go home. It's too good to
lose. It must be by that stile.'

They went to look. Julian still didn't like to put on
his torch, so that it was more a question of *feeling* for
Dick's torch, not looking! Dick suddenly trod on it and
picked it up thankfully.

'Listen, there's that fellow coming back again, I'm
sure!' said Dick. 'I heard the same dry little cough!
What shall we do?'

'Well, I don't now feel like going up to the shepherd's hill to see if that light is flashing from the
tower,' said Julian. 'I vote we hide and follow this chap
to see where he goes. I don't think anyone who is
wandering out tonight can be up to any good.'

'Yes. Good idea,' said Dick. 'Squash into the hedge

again. Blow, there are nettles here! Just my luck.'

The footsteps came nearer, and the cough came again. 'I seem to know that cough,' whispered Dick. 'Sh!' said Julian.

The man came up to the stile, and they heard him climbing over it. After a short time both boys followed cautiously. They couldn't hear the man's footsteps across the grass, but the sky had cleared a little and they could just make out a moving shadow ahead of them.

They followed him at a distance, holding their breath whenever they kicked against a stone or cracked a twig beneath their feet. Now and again they heard the cough.

'He's making for the farm,' whispered Julian. He could just see the outline of the big barns against the sky. 'Do you think he's one of the labourers? They live in cottages round about.'

The man came to the farm-yard and walked through it, trying to make as little sound as possible. The boys followed. He went round the barns and into the little garden that Mrs Penruthlan tended herself. Still the boys followed.

Round to the front door went the man, and the boys held their breath. Was he going to burgle the farm-house? They tiptoed nearer. There came the sound of a soft click, and then of bolts being shot home! After that there was silence.

'He's gone in,' said Julian in amazement.

'Don't you know who it was? Can't you guess now?'

said Dick. 'We both ought to have known when we heard that cough! It was Mr Penruthlan! No wonder he almost dislocated my shoulder with his strong hand!'

'*Mr Penruthlan* – gosh, yes, you're right,' said Julian, astonished, almost forgetting to speak in a whisper. 'We didn't notice that the front door was undone because we went out the back way. So it was he we followed. How silly! But what was he doing out on the hills? He didn't go to see the horse, she wasn't ill.'

'Perhaps he likes a walk at night,' suggested Dick. 'Come on, let's go in ourselves. I feel a bit chilly with practically no shirt on!'

They crept round to the back door. It was still open, thank goodness! They went inside, bolted and locked it, and tiptoed upstairs. They heaved sighs of relief when they were safely in their room again.

'Switch on your torch, Julian, and see if my shoulder is bruised,' said Dick. 'It feels jolly painful.'

Julian flashed his torch on Dick's shoulder. He gave a low whistle. 'My word, you've got a wonderful bruise all down your right shoulder. He must have given you an awful wrench.'

'He did,' said poor Dick. 'Well, I can't say we had a very successful time. We followed our host through the night, got caught by him, and then followed him all the way back here. *Not* very clever!'

'Well, never mind, I bet no light flashed in that tower,' said Julian, getting into bed. 'We haven't lost much by not going all the way to see!'

Chapter Eight

HERE COME THE BARNIES!

THE two boys looked curiously at Mr Penruthlan the next morning. It seemed strange to think of their little adventure the night before with him, and *he* didn't even know it was they he had tried to catch! He gave the curious little dry cough again, and Julian nudged Dick and grinned.

Mrs Penruthlan was beaming at the head of the breakfast table as usual. 'Did you sleep well, all of you?' she asked. 'The storm soon died down, didn't it?'

Mr Penruthlan got up said 'Ah, ock, oooh!' or something that sounded like that, and went out.

'What did he say?' asked Anne curiously. She could *not* think how anyone could possibly understand Mr Penruthlan's extraordinary speech. Julian had said that he thought he must talk in shorthand!

'He said he might not be back for dinner,' said Mrs Penruthlan. 'I hope he'll get some somewhere. He had his breakfast at half past six, and that's very early. I'm glad he came in and had a cup of your breakfast tea now. The poor man had a very bad night, I'm sorry to say.'

The boys pricked up their ears. 'What happened?' asked Julian at once.

'Oh, he had to get up and go and spend two hours with poor Jenny,' said Mrs Penruthlan. 'I woke when he left, but luckily Benny didn't bark, and it wasn't till two hours later he came back, he'd been sitting with the horse all that time, poor man.'

Julian and Dick did not feel at all sympathetic. They knew quite well where Mr Penruthlan had been, not with the horse, that was certain! Anyway, Jenny hadn't been ill when they had looked at her in the night. What a lot of untruths!

They were puzzled. Why should Mr Penruthlan deceive his wife and tell her what wasn't true? What had he been doing that he didn't even want *her* to know?

They told the girls everything immediately after breakfast, when they went to pick currants, raspberries and plums for a fruit salad. Anne and George listened in surprise.

'You never told us you were going,' said George, reproachfully. 'I'd like to have come with you.'

'I always thought Mr Penruthlan looked sort of strange and – and *sinister*,' said Anne. 'I'm sure he's up to no good. What a pity. His wife is so very nice.'

They went on picking the endless red-currants. Anne suddenly got the feeling that somebody was hiding somewhere near. She looked round uncomfortably. Yes, there was someone in the tall raspberry canes, she was sure! She watched.

It was Yan, of course. She might have guessed! He flashed his smile at her and came towards her. He liked Anne best of all! He held out his hand.

'No, I've no sweets,' said Anne. 'How did you get on last night in the storm, Yan? Were you frightened?'

Yan shook his head. Then he came nearer and spoke softly.

'I seen the light last night!'

Anne stared at him, astonished. What light?

'You don't mean – the light that flashes in that old hidden tower?' she said.

He nodded. Anne went quickly to Julian and Dick, who were picking white currants and eating just about as many as they put into the basket!

'Julian! Dick! Yan says he saw that light flashing last night, the one in the tower!'

'Gosh!' said the boys together. They turned to Yan, who had followed Anne. 'You saw that light?' said Julian.

Yan nodded. 'Big light. Very big,' he said. 'Like – like a fire.'

'Shining from the tower?' said Dick, and Yan nodded again.

'Did your Grandad see it?' asked Dick.

Yan nodded. 'He seen it, too.'

'Are you telling the truth?' demanded Julian, wondering how far he could believe Yan.

Yan nodded again.

'What time was this?' asked Dick. But that Yan couldn't tell him. He had no watch, and if he had had, he wouldn't have been able to use it. He couldn't tell the time.

'Blow!' said Julian to Dick. 'We missed it. If Yan's telling the truth we would have seen that light last night.'

'Yes. Well, we'll go tonight and watch for it,' said Dick, determined. 'It's a wild enough day, all wind and scurrying clouds. If that light is used at night in weather like this, we'll be able to see it again. But I'm blessed if I can understand why the wreckers' tower should be used nowadays. No ship would take any notice of an odd light like that when they've got the lighthouse signalling hard all the time!'

'I go, too,' nodded Yan, who had overheard this.

'No, you won't,' said Julian. 'You stay with Grandad. He'll wonder where you are if you're not there.'

It began to rain. 'Blow!' said George. 'I do hope the weather hasn't broken up. It's been so gorgeous. It's quite cold today with this tearing wind. Come on, let's go in, Anne. We've got enough now to feed an army, I should think!'

They all went in, just as the rain came down properly. Mrs Penruthlan greeted them in excitement.

'The Barnies want our barn for tomorrow night!' she said. 'They're giving their first show in our barn, and after that they go to another place. Would you like to help clear out the barn and get ready?'

'Rather!' said Julian. 'We'll go now. There's a lot of stuff to clear out. Where shall we put it? In the other barn?'

The Barnies arrived in about twenty minutes and went straight to the barn, which they had been lent several times before for their shows. They were pleased to see the children and were glad of their help.

They were no longer dressed in fancy clothes, as they had been when the children had seen them on the Sunday evening. They were practically all dressed in slacks, the women, too, ready for the hard work of clearing the barn and setting up a simple stage and background.

Julian caught sight of a horse's head being carried in by a little nimble fellow who pranced along with it comically.

'What's that for?' he said. 'Oh, is that Clopper's head? The horse that can sit down and cross its legs?'

'That's right,' said the little fellow. 'I'm in charge of it. Never let it out of my sight! Guv'nor's orders!'

'Who's the Guv'nor?' asked Julian. 'The fellow over there?' He nodded to a grim-faced man who was supervising the moving of some bales of straw.

'That's him,' said the little man with a grin. 'His lordship himself! What do you think of my horse, chum!'

Julian looked at the horse's head. It was beautifully made and had a most comical look in its eye. Its mouth could open and shut, and so could its big eyes.

'I'm only the hind legs,' said the little man regretfully. 'But I work his tail, too. Mr Binks over there is his front legs, and works his head, the horse's head, I

mean. You should see old Clopper when he performs!
My, there isn't a horse like him in the world. He can
do everything short of fly!'

'Where are his back and front legs – and – er – his
body part?' asked Dick, coming up and looking with
great interest at the horse's head.

'Over there,' said the little man. 'By the way, my
name's Sid. What's yours, and how is it you're here?'

Julian introduced himself and Dick, and explained
that they were helping because they were staying at
the farm. He caught hold of a bale of straw, thinking
it was about time he did some work.

'Like to give me a hand?' he asked.

Sid shook his head.

'Sorry. Orders are I'm not to put this horse's head
down anywhere. Where I go, it goes! I can tell you,
me and Clopper are quite attached to one another!'

'Why? Is it so valuable?' asked Dick.

'It's not so much that,' said Sid. 'It's just that Clopper's so popular, you know. And he's important. You
see, whenever we think the show's flopping a bit, we
bring Clopper on, and then we get the laughs and the
claps, and the audience is in a good temper. Oh,
Clopper's saved the show times without number. He's
a jolly good horse is Clopper.'

Mr Binks came up. He was bigger than Sid and
much stronger. He grinned at the two boys. 'Admiring
old Clopper?' he said. 'Did Sid tell you about the time
Clopper's head dropped off the wagon and we didn't
miss him till we were miles away? My word, what a

state the Guv'nor was in! Said we couldn't give a show without Clopper, and nearly gave us all the sack!'

'We're important, we are,' said Sid, throwing out his chest and doing a funny little strut with the horse's head in front of him. 'Me and Binks and Clopper – no show without us!'

'Don't you put that horse down even for a moment,' warned Mr Binks. 'The Guv'nor's got his eye on you, Sid. Look, he's calling you.'

Sid went over to the Guv'nor, looking rather alarmed. He carried the horse's head safely under his arm.

The grim-faced man said a few sharp words and Sid nodded. Julian went up to him when he came back. 'Let me feel how heavy the horse's head is,' he said. 'I've often wondered, when I've seen something like this on the stage.'

Sid immediately put the horse under his other arm, and glared at Julian, looking round quickly to see if the Guv'nor had heard.

'That's a fool thing to ask me,' he said. 'After I've told you I'm not allowed to put the horse down! And didn't the Guv'nor just this minute say to me "Keep away from those kids, you know what tricks they're up to. They'll have that horse away from you if you're not careful." See? Do you want me to lose my job?'

Julian laughed. 'Don't be silly. You wouldn't lose your job for that! When are you and Mr Binks going to do a bit of practice? We want to see you!'

'Oh well, we could manage that all right,' said Sid,

calming down. 'Here, Binks. Bit of practice wanted. Get the legs.'

Binks and Sid went to a cleared space in the big barn and proceeded to clothe themselves in the horse's canvas skin and legs. Sid showed the boys how he worked the tail with one of his hands when he wanted to.

Binks put on the head and the front legs. His head only went into the neck of the horse, no farther. He was able to use his hands for pulling strings to open the horse's mouth and work its rolling eyes.

Sid got his legs in the horse's back legs, bent over and put his head and arms over towards Binks, so making the horse's back. Somebody came up and zipped up the two halves of the horse's 'skin'.

'Oh! What a jolly good horse!' said Dick, delighted. It looked a lively, comical, extremely supple beast, and the two men inside at once proceeded to make it do ridiculous things. It marched – left-right, left-right, left-right. It did a little tap-dance with its front feet, which then remained perfectly still, and then the back feet did the same little tap-dance.

The back feet got themselves entangled and fell over, and the horse's head looked round at itself in astonishment.

All four children were now watching, and Yan was peeping in at the door. They roared with laughter at the ridiculous horse.

It took its tail in its mouth and marched round and round itself. It stood up on its hind legs only. It jumped like a kangaroo, and made peculiar noises. The whole company stood and watched and even the grim-faced Guv'nor had to smile.

Then it sat down on its hind-legs and crossed its front ones in the air, looking round comically. It then gave an enormous yawn that showed dozens of large teeth.

'Oh, don't do any more!' cried Anne, who was weak with laughing. 'Don't! Oh, I can quite well see how important you are, Clopper! You'll be the best part of the show!'

It was a mad, gay morning, for the Barnies were full of chatter and jokes and laughter. Sid and Binks took off their horse garments, and Sid thereupon went about as before, the horse's head, grinning comically, tucked safely under his arm.

Mrs Penruthlan called the children in to dinner. Yan ran after Julian, and caught hold of his arm.

'I seen that light,' he said, urgently. 'You come, see it tonight. Don't forget. I seen that light!'

Julian *had* forgotten it in the excitement of the morning. He grinned down at the small boy.

'All right, all right. I won't forget. We're coming along tonight, but you're not coming, Yan, so get that out of your head! Look, here's a sweet for you. Now, scoot!'

Chapter Nine

THE LIGHT IN THE TOWER

By the end of the day the big barn was quite transformed! It had been cleared of all straw, sacks of corn, bags of fertilizer and odd machines that had been stored in it. It looked enormous now, and the Barnies were very pleased with it.

'We've been here plenty of times,' they told the children. 'It's the best barn in the district. We don't get the best audience, though, because it's rather a lonely spot here, and there are only two villages near enough to send people to see us. Still, we have a good time, and Mrs Penruthlan gives us a marvellous supper afterwards!'

'I bet she does!' said Dick, grinning. 'I bet that's why you come to this lonely spot, too, to taste Mrs Penruthlan's cooking. I don't blame you. I'd come a good few miles myself!'

A stage had been set up, made of long boards, supported on barrels. A back-cloth had been unrolled and hung over the wooden wall of the barn at the back of the stage. It showed a country scene, and had been painted by the company themselves, bit by bit.

'That's my bit,' said Sid, showing Dick a horse standing in one of the fields painted on the back-cloth. 'I had to put old Clopper in! See him?'

The Barnies had plenty of scenery, which they were used to changing several times during their performance. This was all home-made too, and they were very proud of it, especially some that represented a castle with a tower.

The tower reminded the boys of the one Yan had said he had seen flashing a light the night before. They looked at one another secretly, and Julian nodded slightly. They would certainly watch to see that light themselves. Then they would know for certain whether Grandad and Yan were telling the truth.

Julian wondered if they would have to look out for Mr Penruthlan again that night. Jenny the horse was quite better now, if she had ever been ill, and was out in the fields again. So Mr Penruthlan had no excuse for creeping about the countryside at night again!

Neither of the boys could *imagine* what had taken him out the night before, on such a wild night too! Was he meeting somebody? He hadn't had time to go up to see the shepherd about anything, and there wouldn't have been much point in that anyway. He had seen Grandad in the morning already.

Mrs Penruthlan came to see the barn now that it was almost ready for the show the next night. She looked red and excited. This was a grand time for her, the Barnies in her barn, the villagers all coming up the next night, a grand supper to be held afterwards. What an excitement!

She was very busy in her kitchen, cooking, cooking, cooking! Her enormous larder was already full of the most appetising looking pies, tarts, hams, brawns and cheeses. The children took turns at looking into it and sniffing in delight. Mrs Penruthlan laughed at them and shooed them out.

'You'll have to help me tomorrow,' she said. 'Shelling peas, scraping potatoes, stringing beans, picking currants and raspberries, and you'll find hundreds of wild strawberries in the copse, too, which can go to add a flavour to the fruit salad.'

'We shall love to help,' said Anne. 'All this is grand fun! But surely you aren't going to do all the supper single-handed, Mrs Penruthlan?'

'Oh, one or two of the villagers will stay behind to help me serve it,' said the plump little farmer's wife, who looked as happy as could be in the midst of so much hard work. 'Anyway, I'll be up at five o'clock tomorrow morning. I'll have plenty of time!'

'You'd better go to bed early tonight then!' said George.

'We all will,' said Mrs Penruthlan. 'We'll be up early and abed late tomorrow, and we'll need some sleep tonight. It's no trouble to get Mr Penruthlan to bed early. He's always ready to go!'

The children felt sure he would be ready to go early that night because he had spent so much time out in the storm the night before! Julian and Dick were tired too, but they were quite determined to go up to the shepherd's hill and find the place where they could watch and see if that light really did flash out!

They had a high tea as usual, at which Mr Penruthlan was present. He ate solidly and solemnly, not saying a word except something that sounded like 'Ooahah, ooh.'

'Well, I'm glad you like the pie, Mr Penruthlan,' said his wife. 'Though I says it as shouldn't, it's a good one.'

It really was wonderful the way she understood her husband's speech. It was also very queer to hear her speak to her husband as if he was someone to whom she had to be polite, and call Mister! Anne wondered if she called him Mr Penruthlan when they were alone together. She looked at him earnestly. What a dark giant he was – and how he ate!

He looked up and saw Anne watching him. He nodded at her and said 'Ah! Oooh, ock, ukker.' It might have been a foreign language for all Anne could understand! She looked startled and didn't know what to say.

'Now, Mr Penruthlan, don't you tease the child!' said his wife. 'She doesn't know what to answer. Do you, Anne?'

'Well – I – er – I didn't really catch what he said,' said Anne, going scarlet.

'There now, Mr Penruthlan – see how badly you talk without your teeth in!' said the farmer's wife scoldingly. 'Haven't I told you you should wear your teeth when you want to make conversation? *I* understand you all right, but others don't. It must sound just a mumble to them!'

Mr Penruthlan frowned and muttered something.

The children all stared at him, dumbfounded to hear that he had no teeth. Goodness gracious – HOW did he manage to eat all he did, then? He seemed to chew and munch and crunch, and yet he had no teeth!

'So that's why he speaks so queerly,' thought Dick, amused. 'But fancy eating as much as he does, with no teeth in his head! Goodness, what would he eat if he *had* got all his teeth.'

Mrs Penruthlan changed the conversation because it was clear that her husband was annoyed with her. She talked brightly about the Barnies.

'That horse Clopper! You wait till you see him prance on to the stage, and fall off it. You'll see Mr Penruthlan almost fall out of his seat he laughs so much. He's fair set on that horse. He's seen it a dozen times, and it tickles him to death.'

'I think it's jolly funny myself,' said Julian. 'I've always thought I'd like to put on an act like that at our end-of-term concert at school. Dick and I could do it all right. I wish Sid and Mr Binks would let us try.'

The meal was finished at last. Most of the dishes were empty, and Mrs Penruthlan looked pleased. 'There now – you've done really well,' she said. 'That's what I do like to see, people finishing up everything put before them.'

'It's easy when it's food *you* put before us,' said George. 'Isn't it, Timmy? I bet Timmy wishes he lived here always, Mrs Penruthlan! I'm sure he keeps telling your dogs how lucky they are!'

After the washing-up, in which everyone but Mr

Penruthlan helped, they went to sit down for a while, and read. But the farmer kept giving such enormous yawns that he set everyone else yawning too, and Mrs Penruthlan began to laugh.

'Come on, to bed, all of you!' she said. 'I've never heard so many yawns in my life! Poor Mr Penruthlan. He's tired out with sitting up with Jenny the horse half the night.'

The children exchanged glances. They knew better!

Everyone went up to bed, and the children laughed to hear Mr Penruthlan still yawning loudly in his room. Julian looked out of his window. It was a dark, blustery night, with sudden spurts of sharp rain. The wind howled and Julian almost thought he could hear the great waves crashing on the rocks in the nearest coves! How enormous they would be in this wind!

'A good night for wreckers, if there were any nowadays!' he said to Dick. 'Not much chance for any ship that went too near those coves tonight! They'd be on the rocks, and dashed to pieces in half an hour! The beach would be strewn with thousands of pieces of wreckage the next day.'

'We'd better wait a bit before we go,' said Dick. 'It's really very early. On a bright sunny evening the hills would still be full of daylight, but this stormy evening is very dark. Let's light our candles and read.'

The wind became even stronger, and grew almost to a gale. It made a howling noise round the old farmhouse, and sounded angry and in pain. Not a very nice night to go out on the hills!

'We'll go now, I think,' said Julian, at last. 'It's quite dark, and getting late. Come on.'

They hadn't undressed, so they went down the stairs at once, and out of the back door as before, closing it silently behind them. They made their way through the farm-yard, not daring to shine their torches till they were well away from the house.

They had had a quick look at the front door, when they had stood in the hall. It was locked and bolted! Mr Penruthlan was not out tonight, that was certain.

They walked steadily through the gale, gasping when it caught them full in the face. They each had their warm jerseys on, for it was quite cold, and the wind blew all the time.

Across the fields. Over one stile after another. Across more fields. The boys stopped once or twice to make sure they were right. They were relieved when they came to the great flock of sheep, and knew they must be near the shepherd's hut.

'There's the hut,' whispered Julian, at last. 'You can just see its dark outline. We must go quietly now.'

They stole by the hut. Not a sound came from inside, and no candle-light showed through the cracks. Old Grandad must be fast asleep! Julian pictured Yan curled up with him on their bed of old sheepskins.

The boys went quietly along. Now, they must make for the spot from which the old tower could be seen, and it must be the *exact* spot, for the tower could be seen from nowhere else.

They couldn't find it, or, if they *had* found it, and

were standing on it, they were unable to see the tower far off in the darkness.

'If it didn't happen to be flashing a light, we wouldn't know if we were looking in the right direction or not!' said Julian. 'We'd never see it in the dark. Why didn't we think of that? Somehow I thought we'd see the tower whether it was lighted up or not. We're asses.'

They wandered about a little, continually looking in the direction where they thought the tower should be, but saw nothing at all. What a waste of a long walk!

Then Julian suddenly gave an exclamation. 'Who's that? I saw you there! Who is it?'

Dick jumped. What was this now? Then someone sidled up against them both, and a voice spoke timidly.

'It's me, Yan!'

'Good gracious! You turn up everywhere!' said Julian. 'I suppose you were watching out for us.'

'Iss. Come with me,' said Yan, and tugged at Julian's arm. The two boys went with him, a few yards to the right, then higher up the hill. Then Yan stopped.

The boys saw the distant light at once. There was no doubt about it at all! It flashed continually, rather like a small lighthouse light. Each time it flashed they could see the faint outline of the tower.

'It seems to be some kind of signal,' said Julian. 'Flash – flash-flash-flash – flash-flash – flash. My word, how weird. Who's doing it, and why? Surely there are no wreckers nowadays!'

'Grandad says it's his old Dad,' said Yan, in an awed voice. Julian laughed.

'Don't be silly! All the same, it's a bit of a mystery, isn't it, Dick? *Could* any ship out at sea be deceived and come near to the shore, and be wrecked? It's a wicked night, just the night for great waves to pound a ship to pieces if it came near this coast.'

'Yes. Well, we shall hear tomorrow if there *has* been a wreck,' said Dick soberly. 'I hope there won't be. I can't bear thinking of it, anyway. Surely, *surely* there aren't wreckers here now!'

'If there are, they will be creeping down the hidden Wreckers' Way, wherever it is,' said Julian. 'And watching for the ship to crash to pieces. Then they will collect sacks upon sacks of booty and creep away back.'

Dick felt a chill of horror. 'Shut up, Ju!' he said, sharply. 'Don't talk like that. Now, what are we going to do about that light.'

'I'll tell you,' said Julian, firmly. 'We're going to find that tower and see what's going on. That's what we're going to do! And as soon as ever we can too, maybe tomorrow!'

Chapter Ten

GETTING READY FOR THE SHOW

JULIAN and Dick watched the light for a little longer, and then turned to go back to the farm. The wind was so strong and so cold that even on that summer's night they found themselves shivering.

'I'm glad you found us, Yan,' said Dick, putting an arm round the small, shivering boy. 'Thanks for your help. We're going to explore that old tower. Would you like to show us the way to it?'

Yan shivered all the more, from fright as much as cold. 'No. I'm frit,' he said. 'I'm frit of that tower now.'

'What does he mean, frit?' said Dick. 'Short for frightened, I suppose! All right, Yan. You needn't come. It *is* pretty peculiar, I must admit. Now, go back to your hut.'

Yan shot off in the dark like a scared rabbit. The boys made their way home, not very cautiously, for they felt sure they were the only people out that night. But when they came to the farm-yard they saw something that made them stop suddenly.

'There's a light in the big barn!' whispered Dick. 'It's gone, no, there it is again. It's somebody with a torch, flashing it on and off. Who is it?'

'One of the Barnies, perhaps,' whispered back Julian. 'Let's go and see. We know the Barnies are sleeping in the near-by sheds tonight.'

They tiptoed to the barn and looked through a crack. They saw nothing at first. Then a torch flashed, shedding its light on some of the properties of the Barnies, stacked in a corner, scenery, dresses, coats, and other things.

'Somebody's going through the pockets!' said Julian, indignantly. 'Look at that! A thief!'

'Who is it?' said Dick. 'One of the Barnies pick-pocketing?'

For a moment or two the torch lighted up the back of the intruder's hand in the barn, and the boys stifled an exclamation. They knew that hand! It was covered with black hairs almost as thick as fur!

'Mr Penruthlan!' whispered Dick. 'Yes, I see it's him now. Look at his enormous shadow. What's he doing? He must be mad, walking about at night on the hills, stealing into the barn, going through pockets. Look what he's doing now! Looking in the drawers of that chest the Barnies are going to use in one of their scenes. Yes, he's mad!'

Julian felt most uncomfortable. He didn't like spying on his host like this. What a strange man he was! He told untruths, he crept about at night, he went through people's pockets. Yes, he must be mad! Did Mrs Penruthlan know? She couldn't know, or she would be unhappy, and she really seemed the most cheerful, gay little person in the world!

'Come on,' said Julian, in Dick's ear. 'He's going through everything! Though what he expects to find in the Barnies' stage clothes and properties, I don't know. He's got a kink! Come on, I really don't want to spot him taking something, stealing it. It would be so awkward if we had to say we saw him stealing.'

They left the barn and went gack to the farmhouse, creeping in once more at the back door. They looked at the front door. It was shut, but no longer locked or bolted.

The boys went upstairs, puzzled. What a strange night! The howling wind, the flashing light, the furtive man in the barn, they didn't know what to make of it!

'Let's wake the girls and tell them,' said Julian. 'I feel as if I can't wait till the morning.'

George was awake and so was Timmy. Timmy had heard them going out, and had lain awake waiting for them to come back. He had stirred and had awakened George. She was quite prepared to hear a whisper at the door!

'Anne! George! We've got some news!' whispered Julian. Timmy gave a little welcoming whine and leapt off the bed. Soon Anne was awake, too, and the girls were listening in amazement to the boys' news.

They were almost as surprised to hear about Mr Penruthlan in the barn as to hear about the light actually flashing in the tower.

'So it *was* true what old Grandad said, then?' whispered Anne. 'He *had* seen the light again, I do think it's weird, all this. Julian, you don't think we'll hear of a wreck tomorrow, do you? I couldn't bear it!'

'Nor could I,' said George, listening to the wind howling outside. 'Fancy being wrecked on a night like this, and being dashed on the rocks by those pounding waves. I feel as if we ought to rush off to the coves here and now and see if we can do any rescuing!'

'We wouldn't be much use,' said Dick. 'I doubt if we could even get near the cove on a night like this. The waves would run right up to the road that leads down to it.'

They talked and talked about everything. Then George yawned. 'We'd better stop,' she said. 'We'll never wake up tomorrow morning. We can't go and explore that tower tomorrow, Julian. The Barnies will be here, and we've promised Mrs Penruthlan to help her.'

'It'll have to be next day, then,' said Julian. 'But I'm determined to go. Yan said he wouldn't show us the way. He said he was too "frit"!'

'I feel pretty frit myself,' said George, settling down. 'I should have jumped out of my skin if I'd seen that light tonight.'

The boys stole back to their room. Soon they were in bed and asleep. The wind still howled round the house, but they didn't hear it. They were tired out with their long walk over the hills.

Next day was so busy that it was quite difficult to find time to remember the night's happenings! They were reminded of it by one thing, though!

Mrs Penruthlan was seeing to their breakfast, and making bright conversation as usual. She was never at a loss for words, and chattered all day long either to the children or to the dogs.

'Did you sleep well with that howling gale blowing all night long?' she asked. 'I slept like a top. So did Mr Penruthlan! He told me he never moved all night, he was that tired!'

The children kicked each other under the table, but said nothing. They knew quite a lot more about her husband's nights than she did!

After that they had very little time to think of anything but picking fruit, podding peas, rushing here and there, carrying things for the Barnies, helping them to put up benches, barrels, boxes and chairs for the audience to sit on, and even mending tears in some of the stage clothes! Anne had offered to sew on a button, and at once found herself overwhelmed with requests to mend this, that and the other!

It was an extremely busy day. Yan appeared as usual and was greeted uproariously by Timmy, of course. All the dogs loved him, but Timmy was quite silly with him. Mrs Penruthlan sent Yan on endless errands, which he ran quickly and willingly.

'He may be a bit simple, but he's quick enough when he thinks there's some good food he's going to share!' she said. So it was 'Fetch this, Yan!' 'Do that, Yan!' all day long.

The Barnies worked hard, too. They had a quick rehearsal in which every single thing went wrong; the Guv'nor raved and raged and stamped, making Anne wonder why they didn't all run away and stay away!

First there was to be a kind of concert party such as pierrots give on the beaches. Then there was to be a play, most heart-rending and melodramatic, with villains and heroes and a heroine who was very hardly used. But everything came right for her in the end, Anne was relieved to find!

Clopper the horse was to have no definite performance of his own. He just wandered on and off the stage to get laughs and to please everyone, or to fill awkward gaps. There was no doubt he would do this to perfection!

Julian and Dick watched Mr Binks and Sid doing a small rehearsal on their own in a corner of the farm-yard. How well those back legs and front legs worked together! How that horse danced, trotted, galloped, marched, fell over, tied itself into knots, sat down, got up, went to sleep, and, in fact, did every comical thing that Sid and Mr Binks could think of. They really were very, very funny.

'Let me try the head on, Mr Binks,' begged Julian. 'Do let me. Just to feel what it's like.'

But it was no good. Sid wouldn't let him. Mr Binks had no say in the matter at all. 'Orders are orders,' said Sid, picking up the head as soon as Mr Binks took

it off. 'I don't want to lose my job. The Guv'nor says
if this horse's head is mislaid again, I'll be mislaid, too!
So hands off Clopper!'

'Do you sleep with Clopper?' asked Dick, curiously.
'Having to take charge of a horse's head all the time
must be a bore!'

'You get used to it,' said Sid. 'Yes, I sleep with old
Clopper. Him and me have our heads on the pillow
together. He sleeps sound, does old Clopper!'

'He's the best part of the show,' grinned Julian.
'You'll bring the barn down with Clopper tonight!'

'We always do,' said Mr Binks. 'He's the most important member of the Barnies, and he gets paid the
worst. Shame.'

'Yes, back-legs and front-legs are badly paid,' said
Sid. 'They only count as one player, see, so we get half
pay. Still, we like the life, so there you are!'

They went off together, Sid carrying the horse's
head as usual under his arm. He really was a funny
little man, cheery and silly and gay.

Julian suddenly remembered something at dinner-
time. 'Mrs Penruthlan,' he said, 'I suppose that awful
wind didn't cause any wrecks last night, did it?'

The farmer's wife looked surprised. 'No, Julian.
Why should it? Ships keep right out to sea round these
coasts now. The lighthouse warns them, you know.
The only way any ship could come in now would be to
nose into one of the coves at full tide, and then she'd
have to be very careful of rocks. The fishermen know
the rocks as well as they know the backs of their hands,

and they come into the coves at times. But no other craft come now.'

Everyone heaved a sigh of relief. The flashing light hadn't caused a wreck last night, then. That was a mercy! They went on with their meal. Mr Penruthlan was there, eating away as usual, and saying nothing at all. His jaws worked vigorously up and down, and it was impossible to think he had no teeth to chew with. Julian glanced at his hands, covered with black hairs. Yes, he had seen those hands last night, no doubt about that! Not wielding a knife and fork, but sliding into pockets.

The evening came at last. Everything was ready. A big table was placed in the kitchen, made of strong trestles and boards. Mrs Penruthlan gave the two girls a most enormous white cloth to lay over it. It was bigger than any cloth they had ever seen!

'It's the one I use at harvest-time,' said the farmer's wife, proudly. 'We have a wonderful harvest supper then, on that same table, but we put it out in the big barn because there's not enough room here in the kitchen for all the farm workers. And we clear the table away afterwards and have a dance.'

'What fun!' said Anne. 'I do think people are lucky to live on a farm. There's always something going on!'

'Town folk wouldn't say that!' said Mrs Penruthlan. 'They think the country is a dead-and-alive place, but, my word, there's more life about a farm than any-where else in the world. Farm life's the *real* thing I always say!'

'It is,' agreed Anne, and George nodded, too. They had now spread out the snowy-white cloth and it looked lovely.

'That cloth's the real thing, too,' said Mrs Penruthlan. 'It belonged to my great-great-great-grandmother, and it's nearly two hundred years old! As white as ever and not a darn in it! It's seen more harvest suppers than any cloth, and that's the truth!'

The table was laid with plates and knives and forks, cruets and glasses. All the Barnies had been invited, and there were the children, too, of course. One or two of the villagers were staying as well, to help. What a feast they would all have!

The larder was so crammed with food that it was difficult to get into it. Meat pies, fruit pies, hams, a great round tongue, pickles, sauces, jam tarts, stewed and fresh fruit, jellies, a great trifle, jugs of cream – there was no end to the things Mrs Penruthlan had got ready. She laughed when she saw the children peeping there and marvelling.

'You won't get any high tea today,' she told them. 'You'll get nothing from dinner till supper, so that you can get up a good appetite and really eat well!'

Nobody minded missing high tea with that wonderful supper to come. The excitement grew as the time came near for the show. 'Here come the first villagers!' cried Julian, who was at the barn door to help to sell the tickets. 'Hurrah! It will soon begin! Walk up, everyone! Finest show in the world. Come along in your hundreds! Come along!'

Chapter Eleven

THE BARNIES – AND CLOPPER

WHEN the big barn was full of villagers, and a few more boxes had been fetched for some of the extra children, the noise was tremendous. Everyone was laughing and talking, some of the children were clapping for the show to begin, and the excited farm dogs were yapping and barking at the top of their voices!

Timmy was excited, too. He welcomed everyone with a bark and a vigorous wag. Yan was with him, and George was sure that he was pretending that Timmy was his dog! Yan looked cleaner than usual. Mrs Penruthlan had actually given him a bath!

'You don't come to the show and you don't come to the supper unless you bath yourself,' she threatened. But he wouldn't. He said he was 'frit' of the bath!

'I'll be drowned in there,' he said, backing away from it hurriedly. It was already half full of water for him!

'Frit, are you!' said Mrs Penruthlan grimly, lifting him up and plunging him into the water, clothes and all. 'Well, you'll be fritter still now! Take your clothes off in the water and I'll wash them in the bath when you're clean. Oh, the dirty little varmint that you are!'

Yan screamed the place down as Mrs Penruthlan

scrubbed him and soaped him and flannelled him. He
hit out at her, but she gave him one sound spank on
his small behind, and he stopped very suddenly. He
felt very much at her mercy, and decided not to annoy
her in any way while he was in that dreadful bath!

She washed his ragged pants and shirt, too, and set
them to dry. She wrapped him in an old shawl, and
told him to wait till his things dried and then put them
on.

'One of these days I'll make you some decent
clothes,' she said. 'Little rapscallion that you are!
What a mite of a body you've got. I'll need to feed you
up a bit!'

Yan brightened up considerably. Feeding up was
the kind of treatment he really liked!

Now he was down in the barn, welcoming everyone
with Timmy, and feeling quite important. He yelled
with delight when he saw his old great-grandfather
coming along!

'Grandad! You said you was coming, but I didn't
believe you. Come you in. I'll find you a chair.'

'And what's come over you, the way you look tonight?' said the old man, puzzled. 'What you done to
yourself?'

'I've took a bath. See?' said Yan, sounding proud.
'Iss. I took a bath, Grandad. Same as you ought.'

Grandad aimed a cuff at him, and then nodded to
various people he knew. He had his big old shepherd's
crook with him, and he held on to it even when he sat
down on a chair.

'Well, Grandad, it's nigh on twenty year since we saw you down hereabouts,' said a big, red-faced villager. 'What you been doing with yourself all these years?'

'Minding my business and minding my sheep,' said Grandad, in his slow, Cornish voice. 'Ay, and it'll mebbe twenty years afore you sees me again, Joe Tremayne. And if you want to know summat, I'll tell you this. It bain't the show I'm come for, it's the supper.'

Everyone roared with laughter, and Grandad looked as pleased as Punch. Yan looked at him proudly. His old Grandad was as good as anyone, any day!

'Sh! Sh! Show's going to begin!' said somebody, when they saw the curtain twitching. At once the talking and shuffling stopped, and all eyes turned to the stage. A faded, rather torn blue curtain was drawn across.

There came a chord from a fiddle behind the scenes, and then a gay tune sounded out. The curtain was drawn back slowly, halting on its rings here and there, and the audience gave a long sigh of delight. They had seen the Barnies many times but they never tired of them.

All the Barnies were on the stage, and the fiddler fiddled away as they struck up a rousing song with a chorus that all the villagers joined in most heartily. Old Grandad beat time, banging his crook on the floor.

Everything was applauded heartily. Then someone

called out loudly. 'Where's old Clopper? Where be he?'

And old Clopper the horse came shyly on, looking out of the sides of his eyes at the audience, and being so very bashful that old Grandad almost fell off his chair with laughing.

The fiddle struck up again and Clopper marched in

time to it. It grew quicker, and he ran. It grew quicker still and he galloped, and fell right off the stage.

'Hoo-hoo-hoo-hoo!' roared someone. 'HOO-HOO-HOO-HOO!' It was such an enormous guffaw that everyone turned round. It came from Mr Penruthlan, who was writhing and wriggling in his seat as if he was in great pain. But he was only laughing at Clopper.

Clopper heard the giant of a laugh and put a hoof behind one ear to listen to it. Grandad promptly fell off his seat with joy. Clopper caught his back legs in his front legs and fell over too. There was such a pandemonium of screams and guffaws and yells from the delighted audience that it was surprising the roof didn't fall in.

'Off now,' said a firm voice at the side of the stage. Julian looked to see who it was, as Clopper obediently turned to shuffle off, waving one back leg to the admiring villagers. The voice came from the Guv'nor who was standing where he could watch the whole show in detail. His face was still unsmiling, even after Clopper's antics!

The show was a great success, although it could not have been simpler. The jokes were old, the play acted was even older, the singing was a bit flat, and the dancing not as good as the third form of a girls' school, but it was so merry and smiling and idiotic and good-natured that it went with a terrific swing from start to finish.

As for Clopper, it was his evening! Every time his head so much as looked in on the stage, the audience

rocked with joy. They would, in fact, have been delighted to have had one actor only, all the evening,
and that actor, Clopper, of course. Julian and Dick
watched him, fascinated. How they both longed to try
on those back and front legs, and put on the head, and
do a little 'cloppering' themselves!

'Sid and Binks are awfully good, aren't they?' said
Dick. 'Gosh, I wish we could get hold of legs and a
head and do that act at the Christmas school concert,
Ju! We'd bring the house down. Let's ask Sid if we
can have a shot some time.'

'He won't lend us the head,' said Julian. 'Still, we
could do without that, and just try the legs. I bet we
could think of some funny things to do, Dick!'

Everybody was sad when the curtain went across
the stage, and the show was over. The fiddle struck up
'God Save the Queen', and everyone rose loyally to
stand and sing every word lustily.

'Three cheers for the Barnies!' yelled a child, and
the hip-hurrahing rose to the rafters. Grandad waved
his crook too vigorously and hit a very large farmer on
the back of his neck.

'Now, old Grandad!' said the farmer, rubbing his
neck, 'you trying to pick a fight with me? No, no, I'd
be afeared to take you on, I would. You'd get me by
my hind leg with that crook like you do your sheep,
and down I'd go!'

Grandad was delighted. He hadn't had such an
evening for forty years! Maybe fifty. And now for that
supper. That was what he had really come for. He'd

show some of these sixty-year-old youngsters how to eat!

The villagers went home, talking and laughing. Two or three of the women stayed on to help. The Barnies didn't bother to change out of their acting clothes, but came into the kitchen as they were, grease-paint running down their cheeks in the heat. The barn had got very hot with so many people packed in close together.

The children were simply delighted with every-thing. They had laughed so much at Clopper that they felt quite weak. The play had amused them too, with its sighings and groanings and threats and tears and stridings around. Now they were more than ready for their supper!

The Barnies crowded round the loaded table, crack-ing jokes, complimenting Mrs Penruthlan, smacking everyone on the back, and generally behaving like a lot of school children out for a treat. Julian looked round at them all. What a jolly lot! He looked for the Guv'nor, surely for once in a way he too would be smiling and cheerful.

But he wasn't there. Julian looked and looked again. No, he certainly wasn't there.

'Where's the Guv'nor?' he asked Sid, who was sit-ting next to him.

'The Guv'nor? Oh, he's sitting in solitary state in the barn,' said Sid, attacking an enormous slice of meat-pie laced with hard-boiled eggs. 'He never feeds with us, not even after a show. Keeps himself to him-

self, he does! He'll be having a whacking great tray of
food all on his own. Suits me all right! I never did get
on with the Guv'nor.'

'Where's Clopper – the horse's head, I mean?'
asked Julian. He couldn't see it beside Sid anywhere.
'Is it under the table?'

'No. The Guv'nor's got it tonight. Said he wasn't
going to have it rolled about under the table, or have
jelly or gravy dropped all over it,' said Sid, taking six
large pickled onions. 'My, Mrs Penruthlan is a wonder! Why don't I marry someone like her, instead of
getting thinner and thinner inside Clopper's back-legs?'

Julian laughed. He wondered who was going to
take the Guv'nor's tray into the barn. He noticed that
Mrs Penruthlan was getting one ready, and he went
over to her.

'Is that for the Guv'nor?' he asked. 'Shall I take it
for you?'

'Oh, thank you, Julian,' said the busy farmer's wife,
gratefully. 'Here it is, and ask Dick to carry in a bottle
and a glass for him, will you? There's no more room
on the tray.'

So Julian and Dick together went out to the barn
with the food and drink. The wind still blew strongly
and rain was beginning to fall again.

'There's no one here,' said Julian, looking round.
He set down the tray, puzzled. Then he saw a note
pinned on the curtain. He went to read it.

'Back in an hour,' he read. 'Gone for a walk. The
Guv'nor.'

'Oh well, we'll leave the tray then,' said Julian. He and Dick were just turning to go when they caught sight of something, the back and front legs of Clopper the horse! They stopped, each with the same thought in his mind.

'Everyone at supper! The Guv'nor gone for an hour. Nobody would know if we tried on the legs!'

They looked at one another, and read each other's mind. 'Let's have a go at being Clopper!'

'Come on, quick,' said Julian. 'You be the back legs and I'll be the front ones. Quick!'

They got into them hurriedly, and Julian managed to do up most of the zip. But it wasn't right without the head. Had the Guv'nor taken it with him? Surely not? It would be quite safe in the barn.

'There it is, on that chair under the shawl!' said Dick, and they galloped over to get it. Julian picked it up. It was rather heavier than he had imagined. He looked inside it to see how far his head went in it, wondering how to work the eyes and mouth.

He put his hand inside, and scrabbled about. A lid fell open in the side of the neck, and out came some cigarettes, scattering over the floor. 'Blow!' said Julian, 'I didn't know Mr Binks kept his cigarettes in Clopper. Pick them up, Dick, and I'll put them back. Thanks.'

He put the cigarettes back in the little space, and shut the lid on them. Then he put the head carefully over his own. It felt extremely strange.

'There are eye-holes in the neck,' he said to Dick. 'That's how Mr Binks knew where he was going. I kept wondering why he didn't bump into things more than he did! Now – I'm ready. The head seems to be on firmly. I'll count – one-two, one-two – and we'll walk in time. Don't let's start any funny tricks till we're used to Clopper. Does my voice sound funny inside the neck?'

'*Most* peculiar,' said Dick, who was now bending over so that his back made the horse's back, and his arms were round Julian's waist. 'I say, what's that?'

'Someone's coming, it's the Guv'nor coming back!' said Julian in alarm. 'Quick, gallop out of the door before we're caught.'

And so, to the Guv'nor's enormous surprise Clopper galloped very clumsily out of the barn door just as he was coming in, almost knocking him over. At first he didn't realize it was Clopper, then he let out a loud roar and gave chase.

'I can't *see*,' panted poor Julian. 'Where am I going? Oh thank goodness, it's an empty stable! Quick, let's un-zip ourselves, and you'll have to take this head off for me, I can't manage it myself.'

But alas and alack! The zip got stuck and wouldn't come undone. The boys tugged and pulled but it wasn't a bit of good. It looked as if they had got to be Clopper for the rest of the evening!

Chapter Twelve

A TRIP TO THE TOWER

'Blow this zip!' said Julian, desperately. 'It's got *absolutely* stuck! It's so difficult for us to undo it from the inside of the beastly horse. Oh, this head. I *must* get it off.'

He pushed at the head but somehow or other it had got wedged on him, and Julian felt that short of pulling his own head off he would certainly never get Clopper's off!

The horse sat down, exhausted, looking a very peculiar shape. Julian leaned the head against the wall of the stable and panted. 'I'm so *hot*,' he complained. 'Dick, for goodness sake think of something. We'll have to get help. But I daren't go back to the barn because of the Guv'nor, and we really can't appear in the kitchen like this. Everyone would have a fit, and Sid and Mr Binks would be furious with us.'

'I think we were asses to try this,' said Dick, pulling viciously at the zip again. 'Ugh! What use are zips, I'd like to know. I feel most uncomfortable. Can't you get in some other position, Ju? I seem to be standing on my head or something.'

'Let's go and scout round the kitchen,' said Julian

trying to get up. Dick tried to get up too, but they both fell down on top of one another. They tried again and this time stood up rather shakily.

'It's not as easy as it looks, is it, to be a two-man horse,' said Julian. 'I wish I could get these eye holes in the right place. I'm absolutely blind!'

However, he managed to adjust them at last, and the two boys made their way cautiously and clumsily out of the stable. They went carefully over the farm-yard, Julian counting one-two, one-two, under his breath so that they walked in time with one another.

They came to the kitchen door and debated whether to try and catch someone's attention without going in. There was a fairly large window near by, open because of the warmth of the kitchen. Julian decided to take a look through to see if George or Anne were anywhere near. If so, he could call them outside.

But he reckoned without the clumsiness of the big head! It knocked against the window-frame, and everyone looked up. There were shrieks at once.

'A horse! Farmer Penruthlan, one of your horses is loose!' cried a villager who was helping with the sup-per. 'He looked in at the window!'

The farmer went out at once. Julian and Dick backed hurriedly away and trotted in very good style over the farm-yard. Where now? The farmer saw their moving figure in the darkness and went after them.

Trot-trot-trot went the horse desperately then gallop-gallop-gallop! But that finished them, because the back and front legs didn't gallop together, got entangled and down went the horse! The farmer ran up in alarm, thinking that his horse had fallen.

'Take your knee out of my mouth,' mumbled an angry voice, and the farmer stopped suddenly, astounded to hear a human voice coming from the horse. Then he realised what was happening – it was the stage horse with two people in it! Who? It sounded like Julian and Dick. He gave the horse a gentle kick.

'Don't,' said Dick's voice. 'For goodness' sake whoever it is, un-zip us! We're suffocating!'

The farmer let out a terrific guffaw, bent down and felt for the zip. One good pull and the horse's canvas skin came in half as the zip was undone.

The boys clambered out thankfully. 'Oh – er – thanks awfully, Mr Penruthlan,' said Julian, rather embarrassed. 'We – er – we were just having a canter round.'

Mr Penruthlan gave another hearty roar and went off towards the kitchen to finish his meal. Dick and Julian felt very thankful. They carried the legs and head of the horse cautiously towards the barn. They peeped in at a window. The Guv'nor was there, striding up and down, looking extremely angry.

Julian waited till he was at the far end of the barn, and then hurriedly pushed the legs and head in at the door, as quietly as he could. When the Guv'nor turned round to stride angrily back the first thing he saw was the bundle that was Clopper! He raced over to it at once, and looked out of the door.

But Julian and Dick had gone. They could own up

the next day when things were not quite so exciting!
They slid quietly into the kitchen, feeling hot and
untidy, hoping that nobody would notice them.

George and Anne saw them at once. George came
over. 'What have you been doing? You've been ages
and ages. Do you want any more to eat before everything is finished up?'

'Tell you everything afterwards,' said Julian. 'Yes,
we do want something to eat. I've hardly had a thing
yet. I'm starving!'

Mr Penruthlan was back in his place eating again.
He pointed with his knife at the boys sliding into their
seats. 'Ock-ock-oo,' he said, beginning to laugh, and
added a few more equally puzzling words.

'Oh, they've been to help you catch the horse that
peeped in at the window, have they?' said Mrs Penruthlan, nodding. 'Which horse was it?'

'Clopper!' said the farmer, quite clearly, and gave
a loud guffaw again. Nobody understood what he
meant, so nothing more was said. George and Anne
guessed, though, and grinned at the two boys.

It was a wonderful evening altogether, and everyone
was sorry that it had to come to an end. The village
women and the two girls stacked the dirty dishes and
plates and the boys carried them to the sink to be
washed. The Barnies gave a hand where they could,
and the big kitchen was full of chatter and laughter. It
was very pleasant indeed.

But at last the kitchen was empty again, and the big
lamp turned out. The village women went home, the

Barnies departed. Old Grandad took Yan's hand and went back to his sheep, saying dolefully that he'd 'et a mort too much and wouldn't be able to sleep a wink, so he wouldn't.'

'Never mind. It was worth it, Grandad,' said Mrs Penruthlan, and shut and locked the kitchen door. She looked round, tired but happy. There was nothing she liked better than to spend hours upon hours preparing delicious dishes for people and then see them eaten in no time at all! The children thought she was truly wonderful.

They were soon all in bed and asleep. The Penruthlans were asleep, too. Only the kitchen cat was awake, watching for mice in the kitchen. She didn't like a crowd. She liked the kitchen to herself!

Next day was fair and warm, though a stiff breeze still blew. Mrs Penruthlan spoke to the four children at breakfast-time.

'I'll be busy today cleaning up the mess. How would you like to take a picnic lunch of some of the remains of the supper and stay out all day? It's a nice day, and you'll enjoy it.'

Nothing could be better! Julian had already planned to make his way to the old tower once used by the Wreckers, and explore it. Now they would have all day to do it in!

'Oh, yes, Mrs Penruthlan, we'd love to do that,' he said. 'Let the girls get the picnic stuff ready for us. You've plenty to do!'

But no, Mrs Penruthlan wouldn't let anyone deal

with food but herself. She proceeded to pack up enough food for twelve people, or so Julian thought when he saw her preparations!

They set off together happily, with Timmy at their heels. The four farm dogs accompanied them for some way, tearing on in front and then tearing back trying to make Timmy as mad as they were. But Timmy was sedate, walking along as if to say, 'I'm taking these children for a walk, I've no time to play with you. You're only farm dogs!'

'Do we want Yan with us if he turns up?' asked George. 'Do we particularly want him to know what we are doing today?'

Julian considered. 'No, I don't think we *do* want him with us. We may find out something we don't want him to know, or to spread around.'

'Right,' said George. 'Well, just you send him off, then, if he comes. I'm fed up with him. Thank goodness he's a bit cleaner than he was!'

Yan did appear, of course. He came up silently on his bare feet. Nobody would have known he was trotting behind if it hadn't been for Timmy. Timmy quite happily left George's heels and went to say how-do-you-do to Yan, jumping up at him in delight.

George turned round to see where Timmy was, and saw Yan. 'Julian, there's Yan!' she said.

'Hallo, Yan,' said Julian. 'Buzz off today. We're going somewhere alone.'

'I come too,' said Yan, strutting along behind. He still looked fairly clean.

'No, you don't come too,' said Julian. 'You buzz off. See? Off you go. We don't want you today.'

Yan's face took on a sullen look. He turned to Anne. 'I come too?' he said, pleadingly.

Anne shook her head. 'No, not today,' she said. 'Another time. Take this sweet, Yan, and go away.'

Yan took the sweet and turned away, his face sulky. He disappeared over the field and was soon lost to sight.

The four children and Timmy went on together, glad of their warm pullovers when the wind blew strongly. Julian gave a sudden groan.

'I shall be jolly glad when we've had our lunch,' he said. 'This bag of food is so heavy it's cutting into my shoulders.'

'Well, let's wait till we get to the tower and we can put the bags down,' said Dick. 'We'll do a little exploring before we have our lunch. I should think Mrs Penruthlan meant us to stay out to dinner, tea and supper, the amount she's packed for us!'

They hoped they were going in the right direction. They had looked at a map, and found various lanes which they thought would eventually lead to the tower, and had worked out which was the best direction to take.

Julian had his compass and was going by that, leading them down lanes, across fields, along little paths, and sometimes along no paths at all! He felt sure, however, that they were going right. They were making for the coast, anyway.

'Look, there are two hills side by side, or cliffs, are they?' said Anne, pointing. 'I believe they are the hills between which we saw that tower.'

'Yes, you're right,' said Dick. 'We're nearly there. I wonder how people got there when the tower and the house were lived in. There appears to be no proper road at all.'

They walked on, over a rough field. They soon found themselves in a very narrow, overgrown lane, deep-set between hedges that almost met overhead.

'A green tunnel,' said Anne, pleased. 'Look out for those enormous nettles, Ju.'

At the end of the lane an overgrown path swung sharply right, and there, not far from them, was the tower! They stood and stared at it. This was where the light had flashed a hundred years ago to bring ships to their doom, and where the light had flashed only the other night.

'The tower's falling into ruin,' said Dick. 'Large pieces have dropped out of it. And I should think the house is in ruin, too, though we can't see enough of it at the moment, just a bit of the roof. Come on. This is going to be fun!'

The tower didn't look the frightening thing it had seemed on the stormy night when the boys saw the flashing light. It just looked a poor old ruin. They made their way to it through high thistles, nettles and willow-herb.

'Doesn't *look* as if anyone has been here for years,' said Julian, rather puzzled. 'I rather wish we'd brought a scythe to cut down these enormous weeds! We can hardly get through them. I'm stung all over with nettles, too.'

They came to the house at last, and a poor, tumble-down ruin it was! The doors had fallen in, the windows were out of shape, and had no glass, the roof was full of holes. An enormous climbing rose rambled everywhere, throwing masses of old-fashioned white roses over walls and roof to hide the ugliness of the ruin.

Only the tower seemed still strong, except at the top, where parts of the wall had crumbled away and fallen. Julian forced his way through the broken doorway into the house. Weeds grew in the floor.

'There's a stone stairway going up the tower!' he called. 'And I say, look here! What's this on each stair?'

'Oil,' said George. 'Someone's been carrying oil up in a can, or a lamp, and has spilt it. Julian, we'd better be careful. That somebody may be here still!'

Chapter Thirteen

IN THE WRECKERS' TOWER

DICK and Anne came hurriedly up to the old stone stairway when they heard what Julian and George had said. Oil! That could only mean one thing, a lamp in the tower.

They all stood and looked at the big splashes of oil on each step.

'Come on up,' said Julian at last. 'I'll go first. Be careful how you go because the tower's in a very crumbly state.'

The tower was built at one end of the old house, and its walls were thicker than the house walls. The only entry to it was by a doorway inside the house. In the tower was a stone stairway that went very steeply up in a spiral.

'This must once have been the door of the tower,' said Dick, kicking at a great thick slab of wood that lay mouldering away beside the stone doorway. 'The tower doesn't seem to hold anything but this stone stairway, just a look-out, I suppose.'

'Or a place for signalling to ships to entice them on the rocks,' said George. 'Oh, Timmy, don't push past like that; you nearly made me fall, these stone steps are so steep.'

As Dick said, the tower seemed to hold nothing but a stairway spiralling up steeply. Julian came to the top first and gave a gasp. The view over the sea was astonishing. He could see for miles over the dark cornflower blue waters. Near the coast the churning of the waves into white breakers and spray showed the hidden rocks that waited for unwary ships.

George came up beside him and stared in wonder, too. What a marvellous sight, blue sky, blue sea, waves pounding over the rocks, and white gulls soaring on the stiff breeze.

Then Dick came up, and Julian gave him a warning. 'Be careful. Don't lean on the walls at all, they're crumbling badly.'

Julian put out his hand and touched the top of the tower wall near him. It crumbled and bits fell away below.

Big pieces had fallen away here and there, leaving great gaps in the wall round the top of the tower. When Anne came up also, Julian took her arm, afraid that with such a crowd up there someone might stumble against a crumbling wall and fall from the tower.

George had hold of Timmy's collar and made him stand quite still. 'Don't you go putting your great paws up on the wall,' she warned him. 'You'll find yourself down in the nettles below in no time if you do!'

'You can quite well see what a wonderful place this is for flashing a light at night over the sea,' said Dick. 'It could be seen for miles. In the old days, when sailing ships got caught in the storms that rage round this coast at times, they would be thankful to see a guiding light.'

'But what a light!' said Julian. 'A light that guided them straight on to those great rocks! Let me see now. Are those the rocks near those coves we went to the other day?'

'Yes, I think so,' said Dick. 'But there are rocks and rocks, and coves and coves round here. It's difficult to tell if they are the same ones we saw.'

'The ships that sailed towards the light must have been wrecked on the rocks down there,' said Julian, pointing. 'How did the wreckers get there? There must have been a path from here somewhere.'

'The Wreckers' Way, do you think?' said Dick.

Julian considered. 'Well, I don't know. I imagine that the Wreckers' Way must have been a way leading to the sea from inland somewhere, certainly a way that was convenient for the villagers to use. No. I'll tell you what *I* think happened!'

'What?' said everyone.

'I think, on a stormy night long ago, the people who lived here in this house went up into the tower and flashed their false light to any ship that was sailing out on the waters. Then, in great excitement, they watched it sailing nearer and nearer, perhaps shown up by lightning, perhaps by the moon.'

Everyone imagined such a ship, and George shivered. Poor wretched ship!

'When the ship reached the rocks and crashed on them, the signallers in the tower gave a different signal, a signal to a watcher up there on the hills,' said Julian, pointing behind him. 'A watcher who was standing on the only spot from which the flash could be seen! Maybe the light gleamed steadily to entice a ship in, but was flashed in code to the watcher on the hills, and the flashing said, "Ship on rocks. Tell the others, and come to the feast!"'

'How simply horrible!' said Anne. 'I can't believe it!'

'It *is* difficult to think anyone could be so heartless,' said Julian. 'But I think that's what happened. And then, I think, the people who lived in this house went down from here to the near-by coves and waited for their friends to come along the other way, the Wreckers' Way, wherever that is.'

'It must be a secret way,' said Dick. 'It must have been a way known only to those villagers who *were* wreckers. After all, wrecking was against the law, and so this whole business of showing lights and wrecking ships must have been kept a dead secret. We heard what old Grandad said, that every wrecker who knew the way had to vow he would tell no one else.'

'Old Grandad's father probably lived in this very house, and climbed the stone stairway on a wild night, and lighted the lamp that shone out over the stormy sea,' said Julian.

'That's why Yan said he was "frit" of this tower,'

said George. 'He thinks his Grandad's dad still lights it! Well, we know better. Somebody else lights it, somebody who can't be up to any good either!'

'And, don't let's forget, somebody who may still be about somewhere!' said Julian, lowering his voice suddenly.

'Gosh! yes,' said Dick, looking round the little tower as if he expected to see a stranger there, listening. 'I wonder where he keeps his lamp. It's not here.'

'The oil splashes are on almost every one of the stone steps,' said Anne. 'I noticed as I came up. I bet it's a big lamp. It has to give a light far out to sea!'

'Look, it must have been stood on this bit of the wall,' said Dick. 'There are some oily patches here.'

They all looked at the dark patches. Dick bent down and smelt them. 'Yes, paraffin oil,' he said.

George was looking at the wall on the other side of the tower. She called to the other three.

'And here's a patch on *this* side!' she said. 'I know what happened! Once a ship had been caught by the light and was on its way in, the men with the lamp put it on the *other* side of the tower to signal to the watcher on the hills, to tell him the ship was caught!'

'Yes. That's it,' said Anne. 'But who could it be? I'm sure nobody lives *here*, the place is an absolute ruin, open to the wind and the rain. It must be somebody who knows the way here, sees to the light, and does the signalling.'

There was a pause. Dick looked at Julian. The same thought came into their minds. *They* had seen somebody wandering out in the stormy night, twice!

'Could it be Mr Penruthlan, do you suppose?' said Dick. 'We couldn't *imagine* why he was out here in the storm the first night we came out to watch for the light.'

'No, he's not the man with the light, *he's the watcher on the hills!*' said Julian. 'That's it! That's why he goes out on wild nights, to see if there's a signal from the tower, flashing to say that a ship is coming in!'

There was an even longer pause. Nobody liked that idea at all.

'We know he tells lies, we know he goes through people's pockets, because we saw him,' went on Julian after a few moments. 'He fits in well. He's the man who goes and stands in that special spot on the hills and watches for a light!'

'What does he do after that?' said Anne. 'Didn't we hear that there were no wrecks here now, because of the lighthouse higher up the coast? What's the point of it all, if there isn't a wreck?'

'Smuggling,' said Julian shortly. 'That's the point. Probably by motor boat. They choose a wild night of storm and wind, when they will be neither seen nor heard, wait out at sea for the signalling light to show them all's clear, and then come in to one of these coves.'

'Yes, and I bet the Wreckers' secret way is used by someone who steals down to the cove and takes the smuggled goods!' said Dick, excited. 'Three or four people, perhaps, if the goods are heavy. Gosh! I'm sure we're right.'

'And it's the watcher on the hill who tells his friends, and down they go to the coves together. It's most ingenious,' Julian said. 'Nobody sees the light on the tower except the boat waiting, and nobody sees the signal inland except the one watcher on the hills. Absolutely fool-proof.'

'We are lucky to stumble on it,' said Dick. 'But what puzzles me is this. I'm pretty certain that the man who lights the lamp didn't come the way *we* came – we'd have seen trodden-down weeds or something. We should certainly have found some sort of a path his feet had made.'

'Yes. And there wasn't anything, not even a broken thistle,' said Anne. 'There must be some other way into this old house.'

'Of course there is! We've already said there must be a way for the man who lights the lamp to get down to the coves from here!' said George. 'Well, that's the way he gets here, of course. He comes up the passage from the cove. How stupid we are!'

This idea excited them all. Where was the passage? Nobody could imagine! It certainly wasn't in the tower, there was no room for anything in that small tower except for the spiral staircase leading to the top.

'Let's go down,' said Anne, and began to descend the steps. A slight noise below made her stop. 'Go on,' said George, who was just behind her. Anne turned a scared face to her.

'I heard a noise down there,' she whispered.

George turned to Julian immediately. 'Anne thinks

there's somebody down there,' she said, in a low voice.

'Come back, Anne,' ordered Julian at once. Anne climbed back, still looking scared.

'Would it be the man who does the lamp?' she whispered. 'Do be careful, Julian. He can't be a nice man!'

'Nice! He must be a beast!' said George, scornfully. 'Are you going down, Ju? Look out, then.'

Julian peered down the stone steps. There was really nothing for it but to go down and see who was there. They couldn't possibly stay up in the tower all day long, hoping that whoever it was would go away!

'What sort of noise did you hear?' Julian asked Anne.

'Well, a sort of scuffling noise,' said Anne. 'It might have been a rat, of course, or a rabbit. It was just a noise, that's all. Something's down there, or somebody!'

'Let's sit down for a moment or two and wait,' said Dick. 'We'll listen hard and see if we can hear anyone.'

So they sat down cautiously, George with her hand on Timmy's collar. They waited and they listened. They heard the wind blowing round the old tower. They heard the distant gulls calling, 'ee-oo, ee-oo, ee-oo'. They heard the thistles rustling their prickles together down below.

But they heard nothing from the kitchen at the foot of the tower. Julian looked at Anne. 'No sound to be heard now,' he said. 'It must have been a rabbit!'

'Perhaps it was,' said Anne, feeling rather foolish. 'What shall we do then? Go down?'

'Yes. I'll go first though, with Timmy,' said Julian.

'If anyone is lying in wait he'll be annoyed to see our Timmy. And Timmy will be even more annoyed to see him!'

Just as Julian was getting up, a noise was quite distinctly heard from below. It was, as Anne had described, a kind of scuffle, then silence.

'Well, here goes!' said Julian, and began to descend the steps. The others watched breathlessly. Timmy went with Julian, trying to press past him. He hadn't seemed worried about the noise at all! So perhaps it *was* only a rat or rabbit!

Julian went down slowly. Who was he going to find – an enemy, or a friend? Careful now, Julian, there may be somebody lying in wait!

Chapter Fourteen

THE SECRET PASSAGE

JULIAN paused on the last step of the spiral staircase and listened. Not a sound came from the near-by room. 'Who's there?' said Julian, sharply. 'I know you're there! I heard you!'

Still not a sound! The kitchen, overgrown with weeds and dark with ivy and the white rambling rose, seemed to be listening to him, but there was no answer!

Julian stepped right into the room and looked round. Nothing was there – nobody was there! The place was absolutely empty and quiet. Julian went through a doorway into another room. That was empty, too. The old house only had four rooms altogether, two of them very tiny, and every one of them was empty. Timmy didn't seem disturbed at all, either, nor did he bark as he certainly would have done if there had been any intruder there.

'Well, Timmy, it's a false alarm,' said Julian, relieved. 'Must have been a rabbit, or even a bit of wall crumbling and falling. What are you sniffing at there?'

Timmy was sniffing with interest at a corner near the doorway. He stood and looked at Julian as if he would like to tell him something. Julian went over to see what it was.

There was nothing there except for some rather flattened weeds, growing through the floor. Julian couldn't think why Timmy should be interested. However, Timmy soon wandered away and went all round the place, wondering why they had come to such a peculiar house.

'Dick! Bring the girls down!' shouted Julian up the stone stairway. 'There doesn't seem to be anyone here, after all. It must have been some small animal that Anne heard.'

The others clattered down in relief. 'I'm sorry I gave you all a shock,' said Anne. 'But it did sound like somebody down there! However, I'm sure Timmy would have barked if so! He didn't seem at all disturbed.'

'No. I think we can safely say that it was a false alarm,' said Dick. 'What do we do next? Have our lunch? Or hunt about to see if we can find the entrance to the passage that leads from here down to the coves?'

Julian looked at his watch. 'It's not really time for lunch yet, unless you're all frightfully hungry,' he said.

'Well, I'm *beginning* to feel jolly hungry,' said Dick. 'But, on the other hand, I feel I can't wait to find that passage! Where on earth is the entrance?'

'I've been in all four rooms,' said Julian. 'None of them seems to have anything but weeds in, no old door leading out of the walls, no trapdoor. It's a puzzle.'

'Well, we'll all have a jolly good hunt,' said George. 'This is the sort of thing I like. Timmy, you hunt, too!'

They began to explore the four rooms of the old house. As weeds grew more or less all over the floor they felt that there could be no trapdoor. If there had been, and the man with the lamp used it, the weeds would surely have shown signs of it. But they grew quite undisturbed.

'Listen,' said Julian at last. 'I've got an idea. We'll make Timmy find the entrance.'

'How?' said George at once.

'Well, we'll make him smell the oil drips on the steps, and follow with his nose any others that have dripped in the weeds,' said Julian. 'I don't suppose the lamp dripped only on the steps. It must have dripped all the way from the passage entrance, wherever it is, to the top of the tower. Couldn't Timmy sniff them out? They would lead us to the entrance we're trying to find!'

'All right. But I'm beginning to believe there *is* no entrance,' said George, getting hold of Timmy's collar. 'We've looked over every single inch of this house. Come on, Tim, you've got to perform a miracle!'

Timmy's nose was firmly placed over the oil-drip on the bottom stair. 'Sniff it, Timmy, and follow,' said George.

Timmy knew perfectly well what she meant. George had trained him well! He sniffed hard at the oil and then started up the stone steps for the next oil patch. But George pulled him back.

'No, Tim. Not that way. This way. There must be other oil drips on the floor of the house.'

Timmy amiably turned the other way. He found an oil drip at once, on a patch of weeds growing on the floor. He sniffed it and went on to another and another.

'Good old Timmy,' said George, delighted. 'Isn't he clever, Ju? He's following where the man walked when he carried that lamp! Go on, Timmy, where's the next drip?'

It was an easy, strong-smelling trail for Timmy to follow! He followed it, sniffing, out of one room into another, smaller one. Then into a third, bigger one, which must have been the main room, for it had a very big fire-place. Timmy went straight to the fire-place, his nose to the ground. In fact, he went right into the hearth, and there came to a stop. He looked round at George and barked.

'He says the trail ends here,' said George, in excitement. 'So the entrance to the secret passage must be in this big fire-place!'

The others crowded to the hearth. Julian produced his torch and shone it up the chimney. It was an enormous one, though part of the top of it had now fallen away. 'Nothing there,' said Julian. 'But – hallo – what's this?'

He now shone his torch to the side of the big fire-place and saw a small, dark cavity there, barely big enough for a man to get into. 'Look!' he said, excited, 'I believe we've found it. See that small hole? Well, I bet if we crawl through that we'll find it's the way to the secret passage! Good old Timmy!'

'We shall get absolutely *filthy*,' said Anne.

'You *would* say that!' said George, scornfully. 'Who cares? This may be very important, mayn't it, Ju?'

'Rather!' said Julian. 'If we're on to what we think we are, and that's Smuggling with a big S, it *is* important. Well, what about it? Lunch first, or exploring that hole?'

'Exploring, of course,' said Dick. 'What about letting old Tim go first? I'll give him a leg-up.'

Timmy was hoisted up to the black hole, and disappeared into it with delight. Rabbits? Rats? What were the children after? This was a fine game!

'Now I'll go,' said Julian, and clambered up. 'It's a bit difficult to squeeze into. Dick, you help

Anne and George up next, and then you come.'

He disappeared, and one by one the others also hoisted themselves to the hole and crawled in, too.

The hole was merely an entrance to a narrow stand-ing-place at the side of the chimney. Julian got down from the hole, and stood still for a moment, wondering if this was just an old hiding-place, and not an entrance to anywhere, after all. But then, just to the right of his feet, he saw another hole that dropped sharply down.

He flashed his torch down, and saw iron hand-grips at one side. He called back and told the others. Then he descended into the hole, at first using the grips for his feet and then for his hands as well.

The hole went down as straight as a well. It came to a sudden end, and Julian found himself standing on solid ground. He turned round, flashing his torch.

There was the passage, in front of him! It must be the one that led down to the coves, the one that the man with the lamp must have used long ago, when he went to gloat over the groaning ships on the rocks.

Julian could hear the others coming down the shaft. He suddenly thought of Timmy. Where was he? He must have fallen headlong down the hole and found himself suddenly at the bottom. Poor Tim! Julian hoped he hadn't hurt himself, but as he hadn't yelped, perhaps he had fallen like a cat, on his feet!

He called up to the others. 'I've found the passage. It starts at the bottom of the shaft. I'll go along it a little way and wait for you all to come. Then we can keep together in a line.'

Soon everyone was safely down the shaft. George began to worry about Timmy. 'He *must* have hurt himself, Ju! Falling all that way; Oh, dear, where is he?'

'We'll soon come across him, I expect,' said Julian. 'Now, keep close together, everybody. The path goes downwards pretty steeply, as you might expect.'

It certainly did. In places the four children almost slithered along. Then Julian discovered iron staples fixed here and there in the steepest places, and after that they held on to them in the most slippery spots.

'These iron staples would be jolly useful to anyone coming *up*,' said Julian. 'It would be almost impossible to climb up this passage without something to help the climber to pull himself up. Ah, here's a more level stretch.'

The level part soon became much wider. And then, quite suddenly, it became a cave! The four came out into it in surprise. It was rather low-roofed, and the walls were made of black rock, that glistened in the light of the torch.

'I wish I could find Timmy,' said George, uneasily. 'I can't even hear him anywhere!'

'We'll go on till we come to the cove,' said Julian. 'This must lead us right down to the shore, probably to the very cove where the ships were wrecked. Look, there's a kind of rocky arch leading out of this cave.'

They went through the archway and into yet another passage that wound between jutting rocks, which made it rather difficult to get through at times. Then suddenly the passage divided into two. One fork went meandering off towards the seaward side, the other into the cliff.

'Better take the seaward side,' said Julian. They were just going to take the right-hand passage when George stopped and clutched at Julian. 'Listen!' she said. 'I can hear Timmy!'

They all stopped and listened. George had the sharpest ears of the lot, and she could hear him barking. So could the others after a few moments. Bark-bark-bark! Bark-bark-bark! Yes, it was Timmy all right!

'Timmy!' yelled George, making the others jump almost out of their skins. 'TIMMY!'

'He can't hear you all this way away,' said Dick. 'Gosh, you made me jump. Come on, we'll have to take the cliff passage. Timmy's barking comes from that direction, not this.'

'Yes, I agree,' said Julian. 'We'll go and collect him, and then come back and take the other passage. I'm sure it leads down to the sea.'

They made their way along the left-hand passage. It was not difficult, because it was much wider than the one they had already come down. Timmy's barking became louder and louder as they went down. George whistled piercingly, hoping that Timmy would come rushing up. But he didn't.

'It's funny that he doesn't come,' said George, worried. 'I think he must be hurt. TIMMY!'

The passage wound round a corner, and then once

more divided into two. To the children's surprise they saw a rough door set into the rocky wall of the passage on the left-hand side. A door! How very extraordinary!

'Look, a door!' said Dick, amazed. 'And a jolly stout one, too.'

'Timmy's behind it!' said George. 'He must have gone through it and it shut behind him. Timmy! We're here! We're coming!'

She pushed at the door, but it didn't open. She saw that it was lightly latched, and lifted the old iron latch. The door opened easily and all the four went through into a curious cave beyond. It was more like a low-roofed room!

Timmy flung himself at them as soon as they came through the door. He wasn't hurt. He was so pleased to see them that he barked the place down! 'Woof! WOOOOOF!'

'Oh, Timmy, how did you get here?' said George, hugging him. 'Did the door click behind you? My word, what a queer place this is! It's a storeroom – look at all the boxes and crates and things!'

They looked round the strange cave, and at that moment there was a soft click. Then something slid smoothly into place. Julian leapt to the door and tried to open it.

'It's locked! Somebody's locked it, and bolted it! I heard them. Let us out, let us *out*, I say!'

Chapter Fifteen

LOCKED IN THE CAVE

DICK, George and Anne looked at one another in dismay. Someone must have been lying in wait for them, someone must have captured Timmy and shut him up. And now they were captured, too!

Timmy began to bark when Julian shouted. He ran to the door. Julian was hammering on it and even kicking it.

A voice came from the other side of the door, a drawling voice, sounding rather amused.

'You came at an awkward time, that's all, and you must remain where you are till tomorrow.'

'Who are you?' said Julian fiercely. 'How dare you lock us in like this!'

'I believe you have food and drink with you,' said the voice. 'I noticed the packs on your backs, which I presume contain food. That is lucky for you! Now be sensible. You must pay the penalty of being inquisitive!'

'You let us out!' shouted Julian, enraged at the cool voice with its impertinent tone. He kicked the door again out of temper, though he knew that it wasn't the slightest use!

There was no reply. Whoever it was outside the cave

door had gone. Julian gave the door one last furious kick and looked round at the others.

'That fellow must have been watching us from somewhere. Probably followed us all the way to the old house, and saw the packs on our backs then. It must have been he that you heard down in the house when we were in the tower, Anne.'

Timmy barked again. He was still at the door. George called him. 'Tim! It's no use! The door's locked. Oh dear, why did we let you go into that hole first? If you hadn't run on ahead and somehow got yourself caught, you'd have been able to protect us when those men lay in wait!'

'Well, what do we do now?' said Anne, trying to sound brave.

'What *can* we do?' said George. 'Nothing at all! Here we are, locked and bolted in a cave inside the cliff, with nobody near except the fellow who locked us in. If anybody's got any good ideas I'd like to hear them!'

'You do sound cross!' said Anne. 'I suppose there isn't anything to do but wait till we're let out. I only hope that man remembers we're here. Nobody else knows where we are.'

'Horrid thought!' said Dick. 'Still, I've no doubt that Mrs Penruthlan would raise the alarm, and a search-party would set out to find us.'

'What a hope they'd have!' said George. 'Even if they did trace us to the old tower, they wouldn't know the secret entrance to the passage!'

'Well, let's look on the cheerful side,' said Julian, undoing the pack from his back. 'Let's have some food.'

Everybody cheered up at once. 'I feel quite hungry,' said Anne in surprise. 'It must be past our dinner-time now. Well, anyway, eating will be something to do!'

They had a very good meal and felt thankful that Mrs Penruthlan had packed up so much food. If they were not going to be let out till the next day they would need plenty to eat!

They examined the boxes and crates. Some were very old. All were empty. There was a big seaman's chest there, too, with 'Abram Trelawny' painted on it. They lifted the lid. That was empty too, save for one old brass button.

'Abram Trelawny,' said Dick, looking at the name. 'He must have been a sailor on one of the ships that the Wreckers enticed to the rocks. This chest must have been rolled up on the beach by the waves and brought up here. I dare say this cave was the place where the man who owned that old house took his share of the booty and hid it.'

'Yes, I think you're right,' said Julian. 'That is why it has a door that can be locked. The Wrecker probably stored quite a lot of valuable things here from different wrecks, and didn't want any other Wrecker to creep up from the cave and take them. What a hateful lot they must have been! Well, there doesn't seem anything of real interest here.'

It was very, very boring in the cave. The children

used only one torch because they were afraid that if
they used the others they had brought they might ex-
haust all the batteries, and then have to be in the dark.

Julian examined the cave from top to bottom to see
if there was any possible way of escape. But there
wasn't. That was quite clear. The cave walls were
made of solid rock, and there wasn't a hole anywhere
through which to escape, big or small!

'That fellow said we'd come at an awkward time,'
said Julian, throwing himself down on the ground.
'Why? Are they expecting some smuggled goods tonight? They've signalled out to sea twice already this
week, as *we* know. Hasn't the boat they expected come
along yet? If so, they must be expecting it tonight, and
so we've come at an awkward time!'

'If only we weren't locked in this beastly cave!' said
George. 'We might have spied on them and seen what
they were up to, and might even have been able to
stop them somehow, or get word to the police.'

'Well, we can't now,' said Dick gloomily. 'Timmy,
you were an ass to get caught; you really were.'

Timmy put his tail down and looked as gloomy as
Dick. He didn't like being in this low-roofed cave.
Why didn't they open the door and go out? He went
to the door and whined, scraping at it with his feet.

'No good, Tim. It won't open,' said Anne. 'I think
he's thirsty, George.'

There was nothing for Timmy to drink except home-
made lemonade, and he didn't seem to like that very
much.

'Don't waste it on him if he doesn't like it,' said Julian hastily. 'We may be jolly glad of it ourselves tomorrow.'

Dick glanced at his watch. 'Only half past two!' he groaned. 'Hours and hours to wait. Let's have a game of some sort, noughts and crosses would be better than nothing.'

They played noughts and crosses till they were sick of them. They played word-games and guessing games. They had a light tea at five o'clock and began to wonder what Mrs Penruthlan would think when they didn't turn up that evening.

'If Mr Penruthlan is mixed up in this affair, and it's pretty certain that he is,' said Julian, 'he'll not be best pleased to be told to fetch the police to look for *us*! It's just the one night he won't want the police about!'

'I think you're wrong,' said George. 'I think he'd be delighted to have the police looking for lost children, and not poking their noses into *his* affairs tonight!'

'I hadn't thought of that,' said Julian. How slowly the time went by. They yawned, talked, fell silent, argued and played with Timmy. Julian's torch flickered out and they took Dick's instead.

'Good thing we brought more than one torch!' said Anne.

Half past nine came and they all began to feel sleepy.

'I vote we try to go to sleep,' said Dick, yawning hugely. 'There's a sandy spot over there, softer to lie on than this rock. What about trying to sleep?'

They all thought it was a good idea and went to the sandy spot. It certainly was better than the hard rock. They wriggled about in the sand and made dents for their bodies to lie in.

'It's still hard,' complained George. 'Oh, Timmy darling, *don't* snuffle all round my face. Lie down beside me and Anne and go to sleep, too!'

Timmy lay down on George's legs. He put his nose on his paws and heaved a huge sigh.

'I hope Timmy's not going to do *that* all night,' said Anne. 'What a draught!'

Although they thought they couldn't possibly go to sleep, they did. Timmy did, too, though he kept one ear open and one eye ready to open. He was on guard! No one could open that door or even come near it without Timmy hearing!

At about eleven o'clock Timmy opened one eye and cocked both ears. He listened, not taking his head off George's legs. He opened the other eye.

Then he sat up and listened harder. George woke up when he moved and stretched out a hand to Timmy. 'Tim, lie down,' she whispered. But Timmy didn't. He gave a small whine.

George sat up, fully awake. Why was Timmy whining? Was there something going on outside the door, men passing perhaps, on their way to the cove? Had the light been flashing out to sea and had it brought in the boat the men were waiting for?

She put her hand on Timmy's collar. 'What is it?' she whispered, expecting Timmy to growl when he next heard something. But he didn't growl. He whined again.

Then he shook off George's hand and went to the door. George switched on her torch, puzzled. Timmy scraped at the door and whined again. But he still didn't growl.

'Ju! I believe someone is at the door!' called George, suddenly, in a low voice. 'I believe Timmy can hear a search-party or something. Wake up!'

Everyone awoke suddenly. George repeated her words again. 'Timmy's not growling. That means it's not our enemies he hears,' she added. 'He'd growl like anything at the man who locked us in.'

'Be quiet for a moment and listen,' said Julian. 'Let's see if we can hear anything ourselves. We haven't got Timmy's sharp ears, but we might be able to hear *some*thing.'

They sat absolutely still, listening. Then Julian nudged Dick. He had heard something. 'Quiet!' he breathed. They listened again, hardly breathing.

They heard a little scrabbling noise at the door. Then it stopped. George expected Timmy to break out into a fusillade of barks at once, but he didn't. He stood there with his head on one side and his ears cocked. He gave an excited little whine and suddenly scraped at the door again.

Somebody whispered outside the door, and Timmy whined and ran to George and then back to the door again. Everyone was puzzled.

Julian got up and went to the door himself, his feet

making no sound. Yes, there was most certainly somebody outside, two people, perhaps, whispering to one
another?

'Who's there?' said Julian suddenly. 'I can hear you
outside. Who is it?'

There was dead silence for a moment, and then a
small familiar voice answered softly:

'It's me. Yan.'

'Yan! Gosh! Is it really you?'

'Iss.'

There was an amazed silence in the cave. Yan! Yan
at this time of night outside the door of the very cave
they were locked in! Were they dreaming?

Timmy went mad when he heard Yan speaking to
Julian. He flung himself at the door, barking and
yelping. Julian put his hand on his collar. 'Be quiet,
idiot! You'll spoil everything! Be *quiet*!'

Timmy stopped. Julian spoke to Yan again. 'Yan,
have you got a light?'

'No. No light. It is dark here,' said Yan. 'Can I
come to you?'

'Yes, of course. Listen, Yan. Do you know how to
unlock and unbolt a door?' asked Julian, wondering
whether the half-wild boy knew even such simple
things.

'Iss,' said Yan. 'Are you locked in?'

'Yes,' said Julian. 'But the key may be in the lock.
Feel and see. Feel for the bolts, too. Slide them back
and turn the key if there is one.'

The four in the cave held their breath as they heard

Yan's hands wandering over the stout door in the dark, tapping here and there to find the bolts and the lock.

Then they heard the bolts being slid smoothly back. How they hoped their captor had left the key in the lock!

'Here is a key,' said Yan's voice suddenly. 'But it is so stiff. My hand isn't strong enough to turn it.'

'Try both hands at once,' said Julian urgently.

They heard Yan trying, panting with his efforts. But the key would not turn.

'Blow!' said Dick. 'So near and yet so far!'

Anne pushed Dick out of the way, an idea suddenly flooding into her mind. 'Yan! Listen to me, Yan. Take the key out of the lock and push it under the bottom of the door. Do you hear me?'

'Iss, I hear,' said Yan, and they heard him tugging at the key. There was a sharp noise as it came suddenly out of the lock. Then, lo and behold! it appeared under the bottom of the door, slid through carefully by Yan!

Julian snatched it up and put it into the lock his side. He turned the key, and unlocked the door. What a wonderful bit of luck!

Chapter Sixteen

WRECKERS' WAY

JULIAN flung open the door. Timmy leapt past him and yelped with delight to find Yan standing outside. He fawned on the boy and licked him, and Yan laughed.

'Let's get out of here, quick!' said Dick. 'That man may be along at any moment, you can't tell.'

'Right. Explanations later,' said Julian. He hustled everyone out, took the key from the inside lock and shut the door. He inserted the key into the outside lock and turned it. He shot the bolts, took out the key and put it into his pocket. He grinned at Dick.

'Now if that fellow comes along to see how we are he won't even know we're gone! He won't be able to get in to see if we're there or not.'

'Where shall we go now?' asked Anne, feeling as if she was in a peculiar kind of dream.

Julian stood and considered. 'It would be madness to go back up the passage and into the old house,' he said. 'If there's any signalling going on, and there's pretty certain to be, we shall be caught again. We'd be sure to make a noise scrambling out of that hole in the fire-place.'

'Well, let's take that other passage we saw, the right-hand one,' said George. 'Look, there it is.' She shone her torch on it. 'Where does it lead to, Yan?'

'To the beach,' said Yan. 'I went down it when I was looking for you all, but you weren't there, so I came back and found that door. There is nobody on the beach.'

'Well, let's go down there, then,' said Dick. 'Once we feel we're out of danger's way we can plan what's best to do.'

They went along the other passage, their torch showing them the way. It was a steep tunnel, and they found it rather difficult going. Anne managed to give Yan a squeeze.

'You were clever to find us!' she said, and Yan gave her a smile which she couldn't see because of the dark.

They heard the sound of waves at last and came out into the open air. It was a windy night but stars were shining in the sky, and gave quite a fair light after the darkness of the passage.

'Where are we exactly?' said Dick, looking round. Then he saw they were on the same beach as they had been a few days before, but a good way farther along.

'Can we get back to the farm from here?' said Julian, stopping to consider exactly where they were. 'Gosh! I think we'd better hurry. The tide's coming in! We'll be cut off if we don't look out!'

A wave ran up the sand almost to their feet. Julian took a quick look at the cliff behind them. It was very steep. They certainly couldn't climb it in the darkness!

Would there be time to look for a cave to sit in till the tide went out again?

Another wave ran up, and Julian's feet felt suddenly wet. 'Blow!' he said. 'This is getting serious. The next big one will sweep us off our feet. I wish the moon was out. These stars give such a faint light.'

'Yan, is there a cave we can go to, a cave open to the air, not inside the cliff?' said George, anxiously.

'I take you back by the Wreckers' Way,' said Yan, surprisingly. 'Iss. You come with me.'

'Of course, you said you knew the Wreckers' Way,' said Julian, remembering. 'If it comes out near here, we're in luck's way! Lead on, Yan. You're a marvel! But do hurry, our feet got wet again just then, and at any moment a giant of a wave may come!'

Yan took the lead. He led them into cove after cove, and then came to a larger one than usual. He took them to the back of the cove, and led them a little way up a cliff path.

He came to a great rock. He squeezed behind it and the others followed one by one. Nobody could ever have guessed that there was a way into the cliff behind that rock.

'Now we are in the Wreckers' Way,' said Yan proudly, and led them on again. But suddenly he stopped and the others all bumped into one another. Timmy gave a short, warning bark, and George put her hand on his collar.

'Somebody comes!' whispered Yan, and pushed them back. Sure enough, they could hear voices in the distance. They turned and hurried back. They didn't want to walk into any more trouble!

Yan got to the front and led them back to the big rock. He was trembling. They all squeezed out behind it, and Yan went along the cliff face to a tiny cave, really only a big ledge with an overhanging roof. 'Sssssssssss!' he said warningly, sounding like a snake!

They sat down and waited. Two men came out from behind the rock, one a big man, and one a small one. Nobody could see them clearly, but Julian hissed into Dick's ear: 'I'm sure that's Mr Penruthlan! See how enormous he is!'

Dick nodded. It was no surprise to him to think that the giant farmer should be mixed up in this. The five children held their breath and watched.

Yan nudged Dick and pointed out to sea. 'Boat comes!' he whispered.

Dick could see and hear nothing. But in a few moments he did hear something, the whirr of a fast motor-boat! What sharp ears Yan must have! The others heard the noise, too, through the crashing of the waves on the rocks.

'No light,' whispered Yan, as the noise of the boat grew louder.

'He'll be on the rocks!' said Dick. But before the boat got to the rocks, the engine stopped. The children could just make out the boat now, swaying up and down beyond the barrier of rocks. Evidently it was not going to try and come any farther in.

Now the watchers could hear voices again. The two

men who had come down Wreckers' Way were standing below the big rock that hid the entrance, talking.
One leapt down to a rock farther down, and disappeared. The other man was left standing alone.

'It was the big man who leapt down,' whispered
Julian. 'Where's he gone? Ah, there he is! You can
just see him moving behind that rock down there.
What's he got?'

'A boat!' whispered Yan. 'He has a boat down
there, pulled up high out of reach of the big waves.
There is a pool there. He is going to row out to the
other boat.'

The children strained their eyes to watch. The sky
was quite clear, but the only light they had was from
the stars, and it was difficult to see anything more than
moving shadows or outlines.

Then there came the sound of oars in rowlocks, and
a moving black shadow of a rowing-boat and man
could be seen faintly, going over the waves.

'Does he know the way through that mass of rocks?'
wondered Dick. 'He must know this coast well to risk
rowing out through rocks at high tide in the dead of
night!'

'Why is he doing it?' asked Anne.

'He's getting smuggled goods from the motor-boat,'
said Julian. 'Goodness knows what! There, I've lost
him in the darkness.'

So had everyone. They could no longer hear the
oars either, for the crashing of the waves on the rocks
drowned every other sound.

Beyond the rocks lay the motor-boat, but only Yan's sharp eyes could see it even faintly in the starlight. Once, in a sudden silence of the waves, there came the exchange of voices over the water.

'He's reached the motor-boat,' said Dick. 'He'll be back in a minute.'

'Look! The second man is going down to the cove now, going to help the first one in, I expect,' said Julian. 'What about us escaping through the Wreckers' Way while we've got the chance?'

'Good idea,' said George, scrambling up. 'Come on, Timmy! Home!'

They went to the great rock and squeezed behind it once more into the entrance of the Wreckers' Way. Then, Yan once more leading, they went up the secret passage, flicking on the torch very thankfully.

'Where does the Wreckers' Way come out?' asked Anne.

'In a shed at Tremannon Farm,' said Yan, to the astonishment of everyone.

'Goodness, so it's very nice and handy for Mr Penruthlan!' said George. 'I wonder how many times he has been up on the hills at night, and has been warned by the tower light to go down Wreckers' Way to the cove and collect smuggled goods from some boat or other! A very good scheme, it seems to me, and impossible for anyone to find out.'

'Except us!' said Dick in a pleased voice. 'We got on to it pretty well. There's not much we don't know about Mr Penruthlan now!'

They went on and on. The passage was fairly straight and had probably been the bed of an underground stream at some time. The way was quite smooth to the feet.

'We've walked about a mile, I should think!' groaned Dick, at last. 'How far now, Yan? Shall we soon be back?'

'Iss,' said Yan.

Anne suddenly remembered that nobody knew how it was that Yan had found them that night. She turned to him.

'Yan, how did you find us tonight? It seemed like a miracle when we woke up to find you outside that locked door!'

'It was easy,' said Yan. 'You said to me: "Go away. Do not come with us today." So I went back a little way. But I followed you. I followed you to the old house, though I was frit.'

'I guess you were frit!' said Dick with a grin. 'Well, go on.'

'I hid,' said Yan. 'You went up into the tower a long time. I came out into the room below, and . . .'

'It was *you* we heard scuffling there, then!' said Anne. 'We wondered who it was!'

'Iss,' said Yan. 'I sat down on some weeds in a corner, and waited till you came down, and then I hid again; but I watched you through a hole from outside. I saw you go through the fire-place. One minute you were there. The next you were gone. I was frit.'

'I love that word!' said Dick. 'So it was you who

flattened down that patch of weeds that Timmy sniffed at? Well, what did you do next?'

'I was going to come too,' said Yan. 'But the hole was so dark and black. I stood in the fire-place for a long time, hoping you would come back.'

'Then what happened?' said Dick.

'Then I heard voices,' said Yan. 'I thought it was you all coming back. But it wasn't. It was men. So I ran away and hid in the nettles.'

'What a place to choose!' said George.

'Then I was hungry,' said Yan, 'and I went back to Grandad's hut for food. He cuffed me for leaving him, and he made me work for him all day. He was angry with me.'

'My word! So you've been on the hills all day, knowing we were down in that passage!' said Julian. 'Didn't you say anything to anyone?'

'I went down to Tremannon Farm to see if you were back when it grew dark,' said Yan. 'But you weren't there. Only the Barnies were there, giving another show. I didn't see Mr or Mrs Penruthlan. I knew then that you must still be down in that dark hole. I was afraid the men had hurt you.'

'So you came all the way again in the dark!' said Julian, astonished. 'Well, you've got pluck, I must say!'

'I was very frit,' said Yan. 'My legs shook at the knees like my old Grandad's. I climbed in at the hole, and at last I found you.'

'With no torch to light the way!' said Dick, and

clapped the small boy on the back. 'You're a real friend, Yan! Timmy knew you all right when you came to the locked door. He didn't even bark! He knew it was you.'

'I wanted to save Timmy too,' said Yan. 'Iss. Timmy is my friend.'

George said nothing to that. She was thinking, rather unwillingly, that Yan was a remarkably brave young man, and that she had been silly and unkind to resent Timmy's liking for him. What a good thing he *had* liked Timmy!

Yan suddenly stopped. 'We are there,' he said. 'We are at Tremannon Farm. Look above your heads.'

Julian flashed his torch upwards, and stared. An open trapdoor was just above them.

'The trapdoor is open!' he said. 'Someone came down here tonight!'

'And we know who!' said Dick, grimly. 'Mr Penruthlan and his friend! Where does that trapdoor lead to, Yan?'

'Into a corner of the machine shed,' said Yan. 'When the trapdoor is shut, it is covered with sacks of corn or onions. They have been moved to open the way down.'

They all climbed out. Julian flashed the torch round the shed. Yes, there were the machines and the tools. Well, who would have thought that the sacks he had seen in here the other day were hiding the trapdoor that led to the Wreckers' Way!

Chapter Seventeen

LONG AFTER MIDNIGHT!

A RAT suddenly shot out from a corner of the shed, and tore across to the open trapdoor. Timmy gave a bark and leapt after it. He just stopped himself from taking a header through the trapdoor by sliding along on all four feet and coming to a stop at the entrance.

He stood up and looked down the hole, his head cocked to one side.

'Look, he's listening,' said Anne. 'Is there someone coming, those men, perhaps, with the smuggled goods?'

'No, he's only listening for the rat,' said Julian.

'I tell you what we'll do! We'll shut the trapdoor and pile sacks and boxes and everything on top of it! Then when the men come up, they'll find themselves trapped. They won't be able to get out. If we can get the police in time, they'll be able to catch them easily.'

'Good idea!' said Dick. 'Super! How mad those two men will be when they come to the trapdoor and find it shut! They can't get out the other way because the tide's up.'

'I'd like to see Mr Penruthlan's face when he sees the trapdoor shut, and feels a whole lot of things piled

on top of it!' said Julian. 'He'll make a few more of
his peculiar noises!'

'Ooh – ah – ock,' said Dick, solemnly. 'Come on,
help me with the trapdoor, Ju, it's heavy.'

They shut the big trapdoor and then began to drag
sacks, boxes and even some kind of heavy farm machine on top of the trapdoor. Now certainly nobody
could open it from underneath.

They were hot and very dirty by the time they had
finished. They were also beginning to feel very tired.
'Phew!' said Dick. 'I'm glad that's done. Now we'd
better go to the farm-house and show ourselves to Mrs
Penruthlan.'

'Oh dear, do we tell her about her husband, and
how he's mixed up in this horrid business?' said Anne.
'I do so like her. I expect she's very worried about us,
too.'

'Yes. It's going to be a bit difficult,' said Julian,
soberly. 'Better let me do most of the talking. Come
on, we'll go. Don't make too much row or we'll set the
dogs barking. I'm surprised they haven't yelled their
heads off already!'

It *was* rather surprising. Usually the farm-dogs
barked the place down if there was any unusual noise
in the night. The five children and Timmy left the
machine-shed and made their way towards the farm-
house. George pulled at Julian's arm.

'Look,' she said, in a low voice. 'See those lights up
in the hills? What are they?'

Julian looked. He could see moving lights here and

there up on the hills. He was puzzled. Then he made a guess. 'I bet Mrs Penruthlan has sent out searchers for us,' he said, 'and they've got lanterns. They're hunting for us on the hills. Gosh, I hope all the Barnies aren't out after us too.'

They came to the farm-yard, moving very quietly. The big barn, used by the Barnies for their show, was in darkness. Julian pictured it full of benches, left from that night's show. The memory of Mr Penruthlan turning out the pockets of the clothes left and hunting through the drawers in the chest used by the Barnies, came into his mind.

A sharp whisper made them stop very suddenly. George put her hand on Timmy's collar to stop him growling or barking. Who was this now?

None of the little company answered or moved. The whisper came again.

'Here! I'm here!'

Still nobody moved. They were all puzzled. Who was waiting there in the shadows, and for whom was he waiting? The whisper came again, a little louder.

'Here! Over here!'

And then, as if too impatient to wait any longer, the whisper moved out into the yard. Julian couldn't see who it was in the dark, and he quickly flashed his torch on the man.

It was the Guv'nor, grim-faced as ever! He flinched as the light fell on his face, took a few steps back and disappeared round a corner. Timmy growled.

'Well! How many *more* people wander about at

night here?' said Dick. 'That was the Guv'nor. What was *he* doing?'

'I give it up,' said Julian. 'I'm getting too tired to think straight. I shouldn't be in the least surprised to see Clopper the horse peering round a corner at us, and saying "Peep-bo, chaps!"'

Everyone chuckled. It was just the kind of thing Clopper *would* do if he were really alive!

They came to the farm-house. It was full of light, upstairs and downstairs. The curtains were not drawn across the kitchen window and the children looked in as they passed. Mrs Penruthlan was sitting there, her hands clasped, looking extremely worried.

They opened the kitchen door and trooped in, Yan too. Mrs Penruthlan leapt up at once and ran to them. She hugged Anne, she tried to hug George, she said all kinds of things at top speed, and to the children's dismay they saw that she was crying.

'Oh, where *have* you been?' she said, tears pouring down her face. 'The men are out looking for you, and all the dogs, and the Barnies too. They've been looking for ages! And Mr Penruthlan's not home, either. I don't know where *he* is, he's gone too! Oh, what a terrible evening. But thank goodness you're safe!'

Julian saw that she was terribly upset. He took her arm gently and led her to a chair. 'Don't worry,' he said. 'We're all safe. We're sorry you've been upset.'

'But where have you *been*?' wept Mrs Penruthlan. 'I pictured you drowned, or lost on the hills, or fallen into quarries. And where is Mr Penruthlan? He went out at seven and there's been not a sign of him since!'

The children felt uncomfortable. They thought they knew where Mr Penruthlan was, getting smuggled goods from the motor-boat, and carrying them back with his friend, up the Wreckers' Way!

'Now just you tell me what you've been doing,' said Mrs Penruthlan, drying her eyes, and sounding unexpectedly determined. 'Upsetting everybody like this!'

'Well,' said Julian, 'it's a long story, but I'll try to make it short. Strange things have been happening, Mrs Penruthlan.'

He plunged into the whole story, the old tower, Grandad's tale of the flashing light, their journey to explore the tower, the secret passage to the wreckers' cove, their imprisonment and escape, and then Julian stopped.

How was he to tell poor Mrs Penruthlan that one of the smugglers was her husband? He glanced at the others desperately. Anne began to cry, and George felt very much like it, too. It was Yan who suddenly spoke and broke the news.

'We seen Mr Penruthlan in the cove,' he said, glad of a chance to put in a word. 'We seen him!'

Mrs Penruthlan stared at Yan, and then at the embarrassed, anxious faces of the other children.

'You saw him in the cove?' she said. 'You didn't! What was he doing there?'

'We think, we think he must be one of the smugglers,' said Julian, awkwardly. 'We think we saw him get into a boat and row to the motor-boat beyond the rocks. If so, he – well – he may get into trouble, Mrs Penru—'

He didn't finish, because, to his enormous surprise, Mrs Penruthlan jumped up from her chair, and boxed his ears soundly. He hadn't even time to dodge.

'You wicked boy!' panted Mrs Penruthlan, sounding suddenly out of breath. 'You bad, wicked boy, saying things like that about Mr Penruthlan, who's the straightest, honestest, most God-fearing man who ever lived! Him a smuggler! Him in with those wicked men! I'll box your ears till you eat your words and serve you right!'

Julian dodged the second time, amazed at the change in the cheerful little farmer's wife. Her face was red, her eyes were blazing, and somehow she seemed to be taller. He had never seen anyone so angry in his life! Yan went promptly under the table.

Timmy growled. He liked Mrs Penruthlan, but he felt he really couldn't allow her to set about his friends. She faced Julian, trembling with anger.

'Now you apologise!' she said. 'Or I'll give you such a drubbing as you've never had in your life before. And you just wait and see what Mr Penruthlan will say when he comes back and hears the things you've said about him!'

Julian was much too big and strong for the farmer's wife to 'give him a drubbing' but he felt certain she would try, if he didn't apologise! What a tiger she was!

He put his hand on her arm. 'Don't get so upset,'

he said. 'I'm very sorry to have made you so angry.'

Mrs Penruthlan shook his hand off her arm. 'Angry! I should just think I *am* angry!' she said. 'To think anyone should say those things about Mr Penruthlan. That wasn't him down in Wreckers' Cove. I know it wasn't. I only wish I knew *where* he was! I'm that worried!'

'He be down Wreckers' Way,' announced Yan from his safe vantage-point under the table. 'We put trap-door down over he. Iss.'

'Down Wreckers' Way!' cried Mrs Penruthlan and to the children's great relief she sank down into a chair again. She turned to Julian, questioningly.

He nodded. 'Yes. We came up that way from the beach – Yan knew it. It comes up in a corner of the machine-shed, through a trapdoor. We – er – we shut the trapdoor and piled sacks and things on it. I'm afraid, well, I'm rather afraid Mr Penruthlan can't get out!'

Mrs Penruthlan's eyes almost dropped out of her head. She opened and shut her mouth several times, rather like a goldfish gasping for breath. All the children felt most uncomfortable and extremely sorry for her.

'I don't believe it,' she said at last. 'It's a bad dream. It's not real. Mr Penruthlan will come walking in here at any moment, at any moment, I tell you! He's not down in the Wreckers' Way. He's NOT a bad man. He'll come walking in, you just see!'

There was silence after this, and in the silence a

sound could be heard. The sound of big boots walking over the farm-yard. Clomp-clomp-clomp-clomp!

'I'm frit!' squealed Yan, suddenly, and made every-one jump. The footsteps came round the kitchen wall, and up to the kitchen door.

'I know who that is!' said Mrs Penruthlan, jumping up. 'I know who that is.'

The door opened and somebody walked in. Mr Penruthlan!

His wife ran to him and flung her arms round him. 'You've come walking in! I said you would. Praise be that you've come!'

Mr Penruthlan looked tired, and the children, quite dumb with amazement at seeing him, saw that he was wet through. He looked round at them in great surprise.

'What are these children up for?' he said, and they all gaped in surprise. Why, he was talking properly! His words were quite clear, except that he lisped over his s's.

'Oh, Mr Penruthlan, the tales these bad children have told about you!' cried his wife. 'They said you were a smuggler. They said they'd seen you in Wreckers' Cove going out to a motor-boat to get smuggled goods, they said you were trapped in Wreckers' Way, they'd put the trapdoor down, and . . .'

Mr Penruthlan pushed his wife away from him and swung round on the astounded children. They were most alarmed. How had he escaped from Wreckers' Way? Surely even his great strength could not lift up

all the things they had piled on top of the trapdoor?
How fierce this giant of a man looked, with his mane
of black hair, his shaggy eyebrows drawn over his
deep-set eyes, and his dense black beard!

'What's all this?' he demanded, and they gaped
again at his speech. They were so used to his peculiar
noises that it seemed amazing he could speak properly
after all.

'Well, sir,' began Julian, awkwardly, 'we – er –
we've been exploring that tower – and – er – finding
out a bit about the smugglers, and we *really* thought
we recognised you in Wreckers' Cove, and we thought
we'd trapped you, and your friend, by shutting the
trapdoor and —'

'This is important,' said Mr Penruthlan, and his
voice sounded urgent. 'Forget all this about thinking
I'm a smuggler. You've got things wrong. I'm working
with the police. It was someone else down in the cove,
not me. I've been on the coast, it's true, watching out,
and getting drenched, as you can see, all to no purpose.
What do you know? What's this about the trapdoor?
Did you really close it, and trap those men?'

All this was so completely astonishing that for a moment nobody could say a word. Then Julian leapt up.

'Yes, sir! We did put the trapdoor down, and if you
want to catch those fellows, send for the police, and
we'll do it! We've only got to wait beside the trapdoor
till the smugglers come!'

'Right,' said Mr Penruthlan. 'Come along. Hurry!'

Chapter Eighteen

DICK GETS AN IDEA!

IN the greatest surprise and excitement the five children rushed to the kitchen door to follow Mr Penruthlan. Yan had scrambled out from beneath the table, determined not to miss anything. But at the door the farmer turned round.

'Not the girls,' he said. 'Nor you, Yan.'

'I'll keep the girls here with me,' said Mrs Penruthlan, who had forgotten her dismay and anger completely in this new excitement. 'Yan, come here.'

But Yan had slipped out with the others. Nothing in the world would keep him from missing this new excitement! Timmy had gone too, of course, as excited as the rest.

'What goings-on in the early hours of the morning!' said Mrs Penruthlan, sitting down suddenly again. 'To think that Mr Penruthlan never told me he was working to find those smugglers! We knew it was going on, around this coast, and to think he was keeping a watch, and never told me!'

Julian and Dick had quite forgotten that they felt tired. They hurried over the farm-yard with Mr Penruthlan, Yan a little way behind, and Timmy leaping round like a mad thing. They came to the machine-shed and went in.

'We piled . . . ' began Julian, and then suddenly stopped. Mr Penruthlan's powerful torch was shining on the corner where the trap door was fixed.

It was open! Unbelievably open! The sacks and boxes that the children had dragged over it were now scattered to one side.

'Look at that!' said Julian, amazed. 'Who's opened it? Sir, the smugglers have got out, with their smuggled goods, and they've gone. We're beaten!'

Mr Penruthlan made a very angry noise, and flung the trapdoor shut with a resounding bang. He was about to say something more when there came the sound of voices not far off. It was the Barnies returning from their search for the children.

They saw the light in the shed and peered in. When they saw Julian and Dick they cried out in delight. 'Where were you? We've searched everywhere for you!'

Julian and Dick were so disappointed at finding their high hopes dashed that they could hardly respond to the Barnies' delighted greetings. They felt suddenly very tired again, and Mr Penruthlan seemed all at once in a very bad temper. He answered the Barnies gruffly, said that everything was all right now, and any talking could be done tomorrow. As for him, he was going to bed!

The Barnies dispersed at once, still talking. Mr Penruthlan silently led the way back to the farm-house with Julian and Dick trailing behind. Yan had gone like a shadow. As he was not at the farm-house when they walked wearily into the kitchen, Julian guessed that he had scampered back up the hills to old Grandad.

'Five past three in the morning,' said Mr Penruthlan, looking at the clock. 'I'll sleep down here for an hour or two, wife, then I'll be up to milk the cows. Send these children to bed. I'm too weary to talk. Good-night.'

And with that he put his hand to his mouth and quite solemnly took out his false teeth, putting them into a glass of water on the mantelpiece.

'Oooh – ock,' he said to his wife, and stripped off his wet coat. Mrs Penruthlan hustled Julian and the rest upstairs. They were almost dropping with exhaustion now. The girls managed to undress, but the two boys flopped on their beds and were asleep in half a second. They didn't stir when the cocks crew, or when the cows lowed, or even when the wagons of the Barnies came trundling out into the yard to be packed with their things. They were going off to play in another village barn that night.

Julian awoke at last. It took him a few moments to realise why he was still fully dressed. He lay and thought for a while, and a feeling of dejection came over him when he remembered how all the excitement of the day before had ended in complete failure.

If only they knew who had opened that trapdoor! WHO could it be?

And then something clicked in his mind, and he knew. Of course! Why hadn't he thought of it before?

Why hadn't he remembered to tell Mr Penruthlan about the Guv'nor standing in the shadows, and his whispered message: 'Here! I'm here!'

He must have been waiting for the smugglers to come to him, of course, he probably used local fishermen to row through the rocks to the motor-boat that had slunk over to the Cornish coast, and those fishermen used the Wreckers' Way so that no one knew what they were doing.

The Barnies often came to play at Tremannon Barn, nothing could be easier than for the Guv'nor to arrange for the smuggling to take place then, for the Wreckers' Way actually had an entrance in the shed near the big barn! If a stormy night came, all the better! No one would be about. He could go up on the hills and wait for the signal from the tower which would tell him that at last the boat was coming.

Yes, and he would arrange with the signaller too, to flash out the news that he, the Guv'nor, was at Tremannon again, and waiting! Who was the signaller? Probably another of the fishermen, descendants of the old Wreckers, and glad of a bit of excitement.

Everything fell into place, all the odd bits and pieces of happenings fitted together like a jig-saw puzzle. Julian saw the clear picture.

Who would ever have thought of the owner of the Barnies being involved in smuggling? Smugglers were clever, but the Guv'nor was cleverer than most!

Julian heard the noise outside, and got up to see what it was. When he saw the Barnies piling their

furniture on the wagons, he rushed downstairs, yelling
to wake Dick as he went. He must tell Mr Penruthlan
about the Guv'nor! He must get him arrested! He had
probably got the smuggled goods somewhere in one of
the boxes on the wagons. What an easy way of getting
it away unseen! The Guv'nor was cunning, there was
no doubt about that.

With Dick at his heels, puzzled and surprised, Julian
went to find Mr Penruthlan. There he was, watching
the Barnies getting ready to go, looking very dour and
grim. Julian ran up to him.

'Sir! I've remembered something, something important! Can I speak to you?'

They went into a near-by field, and there Julian
poured out all he had surmised about the Guv'nor.

'He was waiting in the dark last night for the smugglers,' said Julian. 'I'm sure he was. He must have
heard us and thought we were the men. And it must
have been he who opened the trapdoor, sir. When
they didn't come, he must have gone to the trapdoor
and found it shut, with things piled on it. And he
opened it, and waited there till the men came and
handed him the goods. And now he's got them hidden
somewhere in those wagons!'

'Why didn't you tell me this last night?' said Mr
Penruthlan. 'We may be too late now! I'll have to get
the police here to search those wagons, but if I try to
stop the Barnies going now, the Guv'nor will suspect
something and go off at once!'

Julian was relieved to see that Mr Penruthlan had

his teeth in again and could speak properly! The farmer pulled at his black beard and frowned. 'I've
searched many times through the Barnies' properties
to find the smuggled goods,' he said. 'Each time
they've been here I've gone through everything in the
dead of night.'

'Do you know what it is they're smuggling?' asked
Julian. The farmer nodded.

'Yes. Dangerous drugs. Drugs that are sold at enor-
mously high prices in the black market. The parcel
wouldn't need to be very big. I've suspected one or
other of the Barnies of being the receivers before this,
and I've searched and searched. No good.'

'If it's a small parcel it could be hidden easily,' said
Dick, thoughtfully. 'But it's a dangerous thing to hide.
The Guv'nor wouldn't have it on him, would he?'

'Oh no, he would be afraid of being searched,' said
Mr Penruthlan. 'Well, I reckon I must let them go
this time, and I must warn the police. If they like to
search the wagons on the road, they're welcome. I
can't get the police here in time to stop the wagons
going off. We've got no telephone at the farm.'

Mr Binks came up at that moment, carrying Clopper's front and back legs. He grinned at the boys. 'You
led us a fine dance last night!' he said. 'What happened?'

'Yes,' said Sid, coming up with Clopper's ridiculous
head under his arm as usual. 'Clopper was right worried about you!'

'Gosh, you didn't carry old Clopper's head all over

the hills last night, did you!' said Dick, astonished.

'No. I left it with the Guv'nor,' said Sid. 'He took charge of his precious Clopper while I went gallivanting over the hills and far away, looking for a pack of tiresome kids!'

Dick stared at the horse's head, with its comical rolling eyes. He stared at it very hard indeed. And then he did a most peculiar thing!

He snatched the head away from the surprised Sid,

and tore across the farm-yard with it! Julian looked after him in amazement.

Sid gave an angry yell. 'Now then! What do you think you're doing? Bring that horse back at once!'

But Dick didn't. He tore round a corner and disappeared. Sid went after him, and so did somebody else!

The Guv'nor raced across the yard at top speed, looking furious! He shouted, he yelled, he shook his fist. But when he and Sid got to the corner, Dick had disappeared!

'What's got into him?' said Mr Penruthlan, amazed. 'What does he want to rush off with Clopper's head for? The boy must be mad.'

Julian suddenly saw light. He knew why Dick had snatched Clopper's head. He knew!

'Mr Penruthlan, why does the Guv'nor always have someone in charge of Clopper's head?' he said. 'Maybe he hides something precious there, something he doesn't want anyone to find! Quick, let's go and see!'

Chapter Nineteen

MOSTLY ABOUT CLOPPER

AT that moment Dick appeared again, round another
corner, still holding Clopper's head, with Sid and the
Guv'nor hard on his heels. He hadn't been able to stop
for a moment, or even to hide anywhere. He panted
up to Mr Penruthlan, and thrust the head at him.

'Take it. I bet it's got the goods in it!'

Then Sid and the Guv'nor raced up too, both in a
furious rage. The Guv'nor tried to snatch Clopper
away from the big farmer. But he was a small man and
Mr Penruthlan was well over six feet. He calmly held
the horse's head out of reach with his strong right
hand, and fended off the Guv'nor with the other.

Everyone ran up at once. The Barnies surrounded
the little group in excitement, and one or two farm-
men came up too. Mrs Penruthlan and the girls, who
were now up, heard the excitement and came running
out as well. Hens scattered away, clucking, and the
four dogs and Timmy barked madly.

The Guv'nor was beside himself with fury. He began
to hit the farmer, but was immediately pulled away by
Mr Binks.

Then one of the farm-men shouldered his way
through the excited crowd, and put his great hand on
to the Guv'nor's shoulder. He held him in a grip of iron.

'Don't let him go,' said the farmer. He lowered Clopper's head and looked round at the puzzled Barnies.

'Fetch that barrel,' he said to Julian, and the boy got it at once, placing it in front of the farmer. The Guv'nor watched, his face going white.

'You leave that horse alone,' he said. 'It's my property. What do you think you're doing?'

'You say this horse is your property?' said the farmer. 'Is it entirely your property, inside as well as outside?'

The Guv'nor said nothing. He looked very worried indeed. Mr Penruthlan turned the head upside down, and looked into the neck. He put his hand in and scrabbled about. He found the little lid and opened it. Out fell about a dozen cigarettes.

'They're mine,' said Mr Binks. 'I keep them there. Anything wrong with that, sir? It's a little place the Guv'nor had made for me.'

'Nothing wrong with that, Mr Binks,' said the farmer, and put his hand in again. He pulled at the lid, and ran his finger round the hole where Mr Binks kept his cigarettes. The Guv'nor watched, breathing quickly.

'I can feel something, Guv'nor,' said Mr Penruthlan, watching the man's face. 'I can feel a false bottom to this clever little space. How do I get it open, Guv'nor? Will you tell me, or do I smash Clopper up to find it?'

'Don't smash him!' said Sid and Mr Binks together. They turned to the Guv'nor, puzzled. 'What's up?'

said Sid. 'We never knew there was a secret about Clopper.'

'There isn't,' said the Guv'nor, stubbornly.

'Ah, I've found the trick!' said Mr Penruthlan, suddenly. 'Now I've got it!' He worked his fingers about in the space that he had suddenly hit on, behind the place where Mr Binks had his cigarettes. He pulled out a package done up in white paper, a small package, but worth many hundreds of pounds!

'What's this, Guv'nor?' he asked the white-faced man. 'Is it one of the many packets of drugs you've handled round this coast? Was it because of this secret of yours that you told Sid never to let Clopper out of his sight? Shall I open this packet, Guv'nor, and see what's inside?'

A murmur arose from the Barnies, a murmur of horror. Sid turned fiercely on the Guv'nor. 'You made me guard your horrible drugs, not Clopper! To think I've been helping you all this time, helping a man who's only fit for prison! I'll never work with Clopper again! Never!'

Almost in tears poor Sid pushed his way through the amazed Barnies and went off by himself. After a few moments Mr Binks followed him.

Mr Penruthlan put the white package into his pocket. 'Lock the Guv'nor up in the small barn,' he ordered. 'And you, Dan, get on your bike and get the police. As for you, Barnies, I don't know rightly what to say. You've lost your Guv'nor, but it's good riddance, I'll tell you that.'

The Barnies stared after the Guv'nor as he was dragged away by two farm-men, over to the small barn.

'We never liked him,' said one. 'But he had money to tide us over bad times. Money from smuggling in those wicked drugs! He used us Barnies as a screen for his goings-on. It's good riddance, you're right.'

'We'll manage,' said another Barnie. 'We'll get along. Hey, Sid, come back. Cheer up!'

Sid and Mr Binks came back, looking rather solemn. 'We're not going to use Clopper any more,' said Sid. 'He'll bring us bad luck. We'll get a donkey instead, and work up another act. Mr Binks says he couldn't wear Clopper again, and I feel the same.'

'Right,' said the farmer, picking up Clopper's head. 'Get the back and front legs. I'll take charge of old Clopper. I've always been fond of him, and he won't bring any bad luck to *me*!'

There was nothing more to be done. The Barnies said rather a forlorn good-bye. Sid and Mr Binks shook hands solemnly with each of the children. Sid gave Clopper one last pat and turned away.

'We'll go off now,' said Mr Binks. 'Thanks for everything, Mr Penruthlan, sir. So long!'

'See you again when next you're by here,' said Mr Penruthlan. 'You can have my barn any time, Sid.'

The Guv'nor was safely locked up, waiting for the police. Mr Penruthlan picked Clopper up, legs and all, and looked down at the five children, for Yan was now with them.

He smiled at them all, looking suddenly quite a

different man. 'Well, that's all finished up!' he said.
'Dick, I thought you'd gone mad when you went off
with old Clopper's head!'

'It was certainly a bit of a brain-wave,' said Dick,
modestly. 'It came over me all of a sudden. Only just
in time, too, the Barnies were nearly on their way
again!'

They went over to the farm-house. Mrs Penruthlan
had already run across. The girls guessed why, and
they were right!

'I'm getting a meal for you!' she cried, as they came
in. 'Poor children, not a mite to eat have you had
today. No breakfast, nothing. Come away in and
help me. You can turn out the whole larder if you
like!'

They very nearly did! Ham and tongue and pies
went on the table. Anne picked crisp lettuces from the
garden and washed them. Julian piled tomatoes in a
dish. George cooked a dozen hard-boiled eggs at the
stove. A fruit-tart and a jam-tart appeared as if by
magic and two great jugs of creamy milk were set at
each end of the table.

Yan hovered around, getting into everybody's way,
his eyes nearly falling out of his head at the sight of
the food. Mrs Penruthlan laughed.

'Get away from under my feet, you dirty little ruf-
fian! Do you want to eat with us?'

'Iss,' said Yan, his eyes sparkling. 'ISS!'

'Then go upstairs and wash those dirty hands!' said
the farmer's wife. And, marvel of marvels, Yan went

off upstairs as good as gold, and came down with hands that really were almost clean!

They all sat down. Julian solemnly put a chair beside him, and arranged Clopper in such a way that it looked as if he were sitting down too! Anne giggled.

'Oh, Clopper! You look quite real. Mr Penruthlan, what are you going to do with him?'

'I'm going to give him away,' said the farmer munching as hard with his teeth as he did without them. 'To friends of mine.'

'Lucky friends!' said Dick, helping himself to a hard-boiled egg and salad. 'Do they know how to work the back and front legs, sir?'

'Oh yes,' said the farmer. 'They know fine. They'll do well with Clopper. There's only one thing they don't know. Haw – haw-haw!'

The children looked at him in surprise. Why the sudden guffaw?

Mr Penruthlan choked, and his wife banged him on the back. 'Careful now, Mr Penruthlan,' she said. 'Mr Clopper's looking at you!'

The farmer guffawed again. Then he looked round at the listening children. 'I was telling you,' he said, 'there's only one thing these friends of mine don't know.'

'What's that?' asked George.

'Well, they don't know how to undo the zip!' said the farmer, and roared again till the tears came into his eyes. 'They don't know how to – how to – haw-haw-haw-haw – undo the ZIP!'

'Mr Penruthlan now, behave yourself!' said his amused wife. 'Why don't you say straight out that you're giving Clopper to Julian and Dick, instead of spluttering away like that?'

'Gosh, are you really?' said Dick thrilled. 'Thanks most awfully!'

'Well, you got me what I wanted, so it's only right and fair I should give you what *you* wanted,' said the farmer, taking another plate of ham. 'You'll do well with Clopper, you and your brother. You can give us a show one day before you leave for home. Haw-haw – Clopper's a queer one, see him looking at us now!'

'He winked!' said George, in an astonished voice, and Timmy came out from under the table to stare at Clopper with the others. 'I saw him wink!'

Well, it wouldn't be surprising if he did wink. He's really had a most exciting time!

A complete list of the FAMOUS FIVE
ADVENTURES *by Enid Blyton*

All of these titles are also available in a
hard-cover edition published by
Hodder and Stoughton

Do YOU belong to the FAMOUS FIVE CLUB?

Have you got the FAMOUS FIVE BADGE?

There are friends of the FAMOUS FIVE all over the world.

Wear the FAMOUS FIVE badge and you will know each other at once.

If you would like to join the club, send a 15p postal order or postage stamps, but no coins please, with a stamped envelope addressed to yourself, inside an envelope addressed to:

FAMOUS FIVE CLUB
c/o Darrell Waters Ltd
Palmerston House
Bishopsgate
London EC2N 3BB

You shall have your badge and a membership card as soon as possible, and your gifts will be used to help and comfort children in hospital.

These are other Knight Books

Elizabeth Coatsworth

AWAY GOES SALLY
Sally lived on a farm in New England long ago, with her three aunts and two uncles. Her uncles wanted to move to new land where they would own all they could see. One day in winter Sally and her aunts saw the strangest thing they had ever seen – a great team of oxen drawing a little house on runners towards their door! Here was the house in which they could travel to the new land. So off they all went, and met many adventures on the way.

Catherine Storr

THE CATCHPOLE STORY
Jackie, Ruth and young Ben flew to Nice
for a holiday. On the plane they met a
strange and too-friendly woman with blue
hair. On the return journey she was there
again and this time she had a bag identical
to Ruth's Mysteriously they couldn't
escape her even through customs. And
when they got home the children
discovered Ruth's bag was full of jewellery.
Was it an accident? Was it just stage
jewellery? Where would it lead?

Ask your local bookseller, or at your public
library, for details of other Knight Books, or
write to the Editor, Knight Books,
47 Bedford Square, London WC1 3DP